EX LIBRIS

VINTAGE **CLASSICS**

GIGI AND THE CAT

Colette was an intriguing and flamboyant figure. Born Sidonie-Gabrielle Colette in Burgundy in 1873 she moved to Paris at the age of 20 with her husband, the writer and critic, Henry Gauthier-Villars (Willy). Forcing Colette to write, Willy published her novels in his name and the *Claudine* series became an instant success. She escaped her exploitative first husband to live by her pen and work in music-halls as a dancer. Colette had a lesbian love affair with Napoleon's niece, she married three times, had a baby at 40 and at 47, preferring 'passion to goodness', she seduced her teenage stepson. In the meantime she wrote stunning novels that were admired by Proust and Gide – *Gigi, Sido, Chéri,* and *Break of Day.* Colette lived to be over 80. She was the first woman President of the Académie Goncourt and was the first woman in France to be accorded a state funeral.

ALSO BY COLETTE

Fiction

Claudine and Annie

Claudine Married

Claudine in Paris

Chéri

The Last of Chéri

Chance Acquaintances

Julie de Carneilhan

The Ripening Seed

The Vagabond

Break of Day

The Innocent Libertine

Mitsou

The Other One

The Shackle

Non-fiction

My Apprenticeships and Music-Hall Sidelights

The Blue Lantern

My Mother's House

Sido

The Pure and the Impure

COLETTE

Gigi

AND

The Cat

TRANSLATED BY
Roger Senhouse

VINTAGE BOOKS
London

Published by Vintage 2001

21

Gigi copyright © the Estate of Colette 1944
La Chatte copyright © the Estate of Colette 1933

Colette has asserted her right under the Copyright, Designs and
Patents Act, 1988 to be identified as the author of this work

Gigi first published in 1944 by La Guilde du Livre, Lausanne
La Chatte first published in 1933 by Bernard Grasset, Paris
English translation from the Fleuron Edition, Oeuvres Completes de
Colette de l'Académie Goncourt 1949

First published in Great Britain in 1953 by Martin Secker and Warburg

Vintage
Random House, 20 Vauxhall Bridge Road,
London SW1V 2SA

www.vintage-classics.info

Addresses for companies within The Random House Group Limited
can be found at: www.randomhouse.co.uk/offices.htm

The Random House Group Limited Reg. No. 954009

A CIP catalogue record for this book is available from the British Library

ISBN 9780099422754

Penguin Random House is committed to a sustainable future for
our business, our readers and our planet. This book is made from
Forest Stewardship Council® certified paper.

Printed and bound in Great Britain by Clays Ltd, Elcograf S.p.A.

Gigi

TRANSLATED BY
Roger Senhouse

'DON'T forget you are going to Aunt Alicia's. Do you hear me, Gilberte? Come here and let me do your curls, Gilberte, do you hear me?'

'Couldn't I go there without having my hair curled, Grandmamma?'

'I don't think so!' said Madame Alvarez, quietly. She took an old pair of curling-irons, with prongs that ended in little round metal knobs, and put them to heat over the blue flame of a spirit-lamp while she prepared the tissue-papers.

'Grandmamma, couldn't you crimp my hair in waves down the side of my head for a change?'

'Out of the question. Ringlets at the very ends – that's as far as a girl of your age can possibly go. Now sit down on the footstool.'

To do so, Gilberte folded up under her the heron-like legs of a girl of fifteen. Below her tartan skirt, she revealed ribbed cotton stockings to just above the knees, unconscious of the perfect oval shape of her knee-caps. Slender calf and high-arched instep – Madame Alvarez never let her eyes run over these fine points without regretting that her granddaughter had not studied dancing professionally. At the moment she was thinking only of the girl's hair. She had corkscrewed the ends and fixed them in tissue-paper, and was now compressing the ash-blonde ringlets between the heated knobs. With patient, soft-fingered skill, she gathered up the full magnificent weight of finely kept hair into sleek ripples which fell to just below Gilberte's shoulders. The girl sat quite still. The smell of the heated tongs, and the whiff of vanilla in the curling-papers, made her feel drowsy. Besides, Gilberte knew that resistance would be useless. She hardly ever tried to elude the authority exercised by her family.

'Is Mamma singing Frasquita today?'

'Yes. And this evening in *Si j'étais Roi*. I have told you before, when you're sitting on a low seat you must keep your knees close to each other, and lean both of them together, either to the right or to the left, for the sake of decorum.'

'But, Grandmamma, I've got on my drawers and my petticoat.'

'Drawers are one thing, decorum is another,' said Madame Alvarez. 'Everything depends on the attitude.'

'Yes. I know. Aunt Alicia has told me often enough,' Gilberte murmured from under her tent of hair.

'I do not require the help of my sister,' said Madame Alvarez testily, 'to instruct you in the elements of propriety. On that subject, thank goodness, I know rather more than she does.'

'Supposing you let me stay here with you today, Grandmamma, couldn't I go and see Aunt Alicia next Sunday?'

'What next!' said Madame Alvarez haughtily. 'Have you any other *purposal* to make to me?'

'Yes, I have,' said Gilberte. 'Have my skirts made a little longer, so I don't have to fold myself up in a Z every time I sit down. . . . You see, Grandmamma, with my skirts too short, I have to keep thinking of my you-know-what.'

'Silence! Aren't you ashamed to call it your you-know-what?'

'I don't mind calling it by any other name, only . . .'

Madame Alvarez blew out the spirit-lamp, looked at the reflection of her heavy Spanish face in the looking-glass above the mantelpiece, and then laid down the law.

'There is no other name.'

A sceptical look passed across the girl's eyes. Beneath the cockle-shells of fair hair they showed a lovely dark blue, the colour of glistening slate. Gilberte unfolded with a bound.

'But, Grandmamma, all the same, do look! If only my skirts were just that much longer! Or if a small frill could be added!'

'That *would* be nice for your mother, to be seen about with a great gawk looking at least eighteen! In her profession! Where are your brains!'

'In my head,' said Gilberte. 'Since I hardly ever go out with Mamma, what would it matter?'

She pulled down her skirt, which had rucked up towards her slim waist, and asked, 'Can I go in my everyday coat? It's quite good enough.'

'That wouldn't show that it's Sunday! Put on your serge coat and blue sailor-hat. When will you learn what's what?'

When on her feet, Gilberte was as tall as her grandmother. Madame Alvarez had taken the name of a Spanish lover now dead, and accordingly had acquired a creamy complexion, an ample bust, and hair lustrous with brilliantine. She used too white a powder, her heavy cheeks had begun to draw down her lower eyelids a little, and so eventually she took to calling herself Inez. Her unchartered family pursued their fixed orbit around her. Her unmarried daughter Andrée, forsaken by Gilberte's father, now preferred the sober life of a second-lead singer in a State-controlled theatre to the fitful opulence of a life of gallantry. Aunt Alicia – none of her admirers, it seemed, had even mentioned marriage – lived alone, on an income she pretended was modest. The family had a high opinion of Alicia's judgment, and of her jewels.

Madame Alvarez looked her granddaughter up and down, from the felt sailor-hat trimmed with a quill to the ready-made Cavalier shoes.

'Can't you ever manage to keep your legs together? When you stand like that, the Seine could flow between them. You haven't the shadow of a stomach, and yet you somehow contrive to stick it out. And don't forget your gloves, I beg of you.'

Gilberte's every posture was still governed by the unconcern of childish innocence. At times she looked like Robin Hood, at others like a carved angel, or again like a boy in skirts; but she seldom resembled a nearly grown up girl. 'How can you expect to be put into long skirts, when you haven't the sense of a child of eight?' Madame Alvarez asked. And Andrée sighed, 'I find Gilberte so discourag-

ing.' To which Gilberte answered quietly, 'If you didn't
find *me* discouraging, then you'd find something else.' For
she was sweet and gentle, resigned to a stay-at-home life
and seeing few people outside the family. As for her
features, no one could yet predict their final mould. A
large mouth, which showed beautiful strong white teeth
when she laughed, no chin to speak of, and, between high
cheekbones, a nose – 'Heavens, where did she get that
button?' whispered her mother under her breath. 'If you
can't answer that question, my girl, who can?' retorted
Madame Alvarez. Whereupon Andrée, who had become
prudish too late in life and disgruntled too soon, relapsed
into silence, automatically stroking her sensitive larynx.
'Gigi is just a bundle of raw material,' Aunt Alicia affirmed.
'It may turn out very well – and, just as easily, all wrong.'

'Grandmamma, there's the bell! I'll open the door on
my way out.'

'Grandmamma,' she shouted from the passage, 'it's
Uncle Gaston! !'

She came back into the room with a tall, youngish-look-
ing man, her arm linked through his, chattering to him
with the childish pomposity of a schoolgirl out of class.

'What a pity it is, Tonton, that I've got to desert you so
soon! Grandmamma wishes me to pay a call on Aunt
Alicia. Which motor-car are you out in today? Did you
come in the new four-seater de Dion-Bouton with the
collapsible hood? I hear it can be driven simply with one
hand! Goodness, Tonton, those are smart gloves, and no
mistake! So you've had a row with Liane, Tonton?'

'Gilberte!' scolded Madame Alvarez. 'What business of
yours can that be?'

'But Grandmamma, everybody knows about it. The
whole story came out in *Gil Blas*. It began: *A secret bitterness is seeping into the sweet product of the sugar beet* ...
At school, all the girls were asking me about it, for of
course they know I know you. And I can tell you, Tonton,
there's not a soul at school who takes Liane's side! They
all agree that she's behaved disgracefully! '

'Gilberte!' repeated Madame Alvarez. 'Say goodbye to Monsieur Lachaille, and run along!'

'Leave her alone, poor child,' Gaston Lachaille sighed. 'She, at any rate, intends no harm. And it's perfectly true that all's over between Liane and me. You're off to Aunt Alicia's, Gigi? Take my motor-car and send it back for me.'

Gilberte gave a little cry, a jump for joy, and hugged Lachaille.

'Thank you, Tonton! Just think of Aunt Alicia's face! The concierge's eyes will be popping from her head!'

Off she went, with the clatter of a young filly not yet shod.

'You spoil her, Gaston,' said Madame Alvarez.

But in this she was not altogether speaking the truth. Gaston Lachaille did not know how to 'spoil' anyone – even himself. His luxuries were cut and dried: motor-cars, a dreary mansion on the Parc Monceau, Liane's monthly allowance and birthday jewels, champagne and baccarat at Deauville in the summer, at Monte Carlo in the winter. From time to time he would drop a fat cheque into some charity fund, or finance a new daily paper, or buy a yacht only to resell it almost at once to some Central European monarch: yet from none of this did he get any fun. He would say, as he looked at himself in the glass, 'That's the face of a man who is branded.' Because of his rather long nose and large dark eyes he was regarded on all sides as easy game. His commercial instinct and rich man's caution stood him in good stead, however; no one had succeeded in robbing him of his pearl studs, of his massive gold or silver cigarette-cases encrusted with precious stones, of his dark sable-lined top coat.

From the window he watched his motor-car start up. That year, fashionable automobiles were being built with a slightly higher body and a rather wider top, to accommodate the exaggerated hats affected by Caroline Otero, Liane de Pougy, and other conspicuous figures of 1899: and, in consequence, they would sway gently at every turn of the wheel.

'Mamita,' said Gaston Lachaille, 'you wouldn't make me
a cup of camomile?'

'Two rather than one,' answered Madame Alvarez. 'Sit
down, my poor Gaston.'

From the depths of a dilapidated armchair she removed
some crumpled illustrated papers, a stocking waiting to be
darned, and a box of liquorice allsorts, known as *agents de
change*. The jilted man settled down into it luxuriously,
while his hostess put out the tray and two cups.

'Why does the camomile they brew at home always smell
of faded chrysanthemums?' sighed Gaston.

'It's simply a matter of taking pains. You may not
believe it, Gaston, but I often picked my best camomile
flowers in Paris, on waste ground, insignificant little
flowers you would hardly notice. But they have a taste that
is *unesteemable*. My goodness, what beautiful cloth your
suit is made of! That deep-woven stripe is as smart as can
be. Just the sort of material your father liked! But, I must
confess, he would never have carried it with such dis-
tinction.'

Never more than once during the course of a conversation did Madame Alvarez evoke the memory of an elder
Lachaille, whom she claimed to have known intimately.
From her former relationship, real or invented, she drew
no advantage other than the close friendship of Gaston
Lachaille, and the pleasure to be derived from watching
a rich man enjoying the comforts of the poor when he made
himself at home in her old armchair. Under their gas-
blackened ceiling, these three feminine creatures never
asked him for pearls, chinchillas, or solitaire diamonds,
and they knew how to converse with tact and due solemnity
on scandalous topics traditional and recondite. From the
age of twelve, Gigi had known that Madame Otero's string
of large black pearls were 'dipped' – that is to say, artifici-
ally tinted – while the three strings of her matchlessly
graded pearl necklace were worth 'a king's ransom'; that
Madame de Pougy's seven rows lacked 'life'; that Eugénie
Fougère's famous diamond bolero was quite worthless;

and that no self-respecting woman gadded about, like Madame Antokolski, in a coupé upholstered in mauve satin. She had obediently broken her friendship with a school friend, Lydia Poret, after the girl had shown her a solitaire, set as a ring, the gift of Baron Ephraim.

'A solitaire!' Madame Alvarez had exclaimed. 'For a girl of fifteen! Her mother must be mad!'

'But Grandmamma,' pleaded Gigi, 'it's not Lydia's fault if the Baron gave it to her!'

'Silence! I'm not blaming the Baron. The Baron knows what is expected of him. But plain common-sense should have told the mother to put the ring in a safe at the Bank, while waiting.'

'While waiting for what, Grandmamma?'

'To see how things turn out.'

'Why not in her jewel-case?'

'Because one never knows. Especially as the Baron is the sort of man who might change his mind. If, on the other hand, he has declared himself openly, Madame Poret has only to withdraw her daughter from her studies. Until the matter has been properly cleared up, you will oblige me by not walking home with that little Poret. Whoever heard of such a thing!'

'But supposing she marries, Grandmamma?'

'Marries? Marries whom, pray?'

'Why, the Baron!'

Madame Alvarez and her daughter exchanged glances of stupefaction. 'I find the child so discouraging,' Andrée had murmured. 'She comes from another planet.'

'My poor Gaston,' said Madame Alvarez, 'is it really true, then, that you have broken with her? In some ways it may be the best thing for you; but in others I'm sure you must find it most upsetting. Whom can one trust, I ask you!'

Poor Gaston listened while he drank the scalding camomile. The taste of it gave him as much comfort as the sight of the plaster rose on the ceiling, still black from the hanging lamp now 'converted to electricity', and still faith-

fully retaining its shade – a vast frilly bell of palest green.
Half the contents of a work-basket lay strewn over the
dining-room table, from which Gilberte had forgotten to
remove her copy-book. Above the upright piano hung an
enlarged photograph of Gilberte at eight months, as a
pendant to a portrait in oils of Andrée, dressed for her part
in *Si j'étais Roi*. The perfectly inoffensive untidiness, the
ray of spring sunshine coming through the point-lace curtains, the warmth given out by a little stove kept at a low
heat – all these homely things were like so many soothing
potions to the nerves of a jilted and lonely millionaire.

'Are you positively in torment, my poor Gaston?'

'To be exact, I'm not in torment. I'm just very upset,
as you say.'

'I have no wish to appear inquisitive,' said Madame
Alvarez, 'but how did it all happen? I've read the papers,
of course; but can one believe what they say?'

Lachaille tugged at his small waxed moustache, and ran
his fingers over his thick, cropped hair.

'Oh, much the same as on previous occasions. She waited
for her birthday present, then off she trotted. And, into the
bargain, she must needs go and bury herself in such a
wretched little hole in Normandy – so stupid of her! Any
fool could have discovered that there were only two rooms
at the inn, one occupied by Liane, the other by Sandomir,
a skating-instructor from the *Palais de Glace*.'

'He's Polaire's tea-time waltzing-partner, isn't he? Oh,
women don't know where to draw the line nowadays. And
just after her birthday, too! Oh, it's so tactless! What
could be more unladylike!'

Madame Alvarez stirred the tea-spoon round and round
in her cup, her little finger in the air. When she lowered
her gaze, her lids did not quite cover her protuberant eye-
balls, and her resemblance to George Sand became
marked.

'I'd given her a rope,' said Gaston Lachaille. 'What you
might call a rope – thirty-seven pearls. The middle one as
big as the ball of my thumb.'

He held out his white, beautifully manicured thumb, to which Madame Alvarez accorded the admiration due to a middle pearl.

'You certainly know how to do things in style,' she said. 'You come out of it extremely well, Gaston.'

'I came out of it with a pair of horns, certainly.'

Madame Alvarez did not seem to have heard him.

'If I were you, Gaston, I should try to get your own back on her. I should take up with some society lady.'

'That's a nice pill to offer me,' said Lachaille, who was absent-mindedly helping himself to the *agents de change*.

'Yes indeed, I might even say that sometimes the cure may prove worse than the disease,' Madame Alvarez continued, tactfully agreeing with him. 'Out of the frying-pan into the fire.' After which she respected Gaston Lachaille's silence.

The muffled sounds of a piano penetrated through the ceiling. Without a word, the visitor held out his empty cup, and Madame Alvarez refilled it.

'Is the family all right? What news of Aunt Alicia?'

'Oh, my sister, you know, is always the same. She's smart enough to keep herself to herself. She says she would rather live in a splendid past than an ugly present. Her King of Spain, her Milan of Serbia, her Khedive, her rajahs by the half-dozen – or so she would have you believe! She is very considerate to Gigi. She finds her a trifle backward for her age, as indeed she is, and puts her through her paces. Last week, for instance, she taught her how to eat *homard à l'Américaine* in faultless style.'

'Whatever for?'

'Alicia says it will be extremely useful. The three great stumbling-blocks in a girl's education, she says, are *homard à l'Américaine*, a boiled egg, and asparagus. Shoddy table manners, she says, have broken up many a happy home.'

'That has been known,' said Lachaille dreamily.

'Oh, Alicia is no fool! And it's just what Gigi requires – she is so greedy! If only her brain worked as well as her jaws! But she might well be a child of ten. And what

breathtaking scheme have you got for the Battle of
Flowers? Are you going to dazzle us again this year?'

'Oh Lord, no!' groaned Gaston. 'I shall take advantage
of my misfortune, and save on the red roses this year.'

Madame Alvarez wrung her hands.

'Oh, Gaston, you mustn't do that! If you're not there,
the procession will look like a funeral!'

'I don't care what it looks like,' said Gaston gloomily.

'You're never going to leave the prize banner to people
like Valérie Cheniaguine? Oh, Gaston, we can't allow
that!'

'You will have to. Valérie can very well afford it.'

'Especially since she does it on the cheap. Gaston, do
you know where she went for the ten thousand bunches
thrown last year? She had three women tying them up for
two days and two nights, and the flowers were bought in
the market! In the market! Only the four wheels, and the
coachman's whip, and the harness trappings bore the hall-
mark of Lachaume.'

'That's a dodge to remember!' said Lachaille, cheering
up. 'Good Lord! I've finished the liquorice!'

The tap-tap of Gilberte's marching footsteps could be
heard crossing the outer room.

'Back already!' said Madame Alvarez. 'What's the meaning of this?'

'The meaning,' said the girl, 'is that Aunt Alicia wasn't
in good form. But I've been out in Tonton's "tuf-tuf".'

Her lips parted in a bright smile.

'You know, Tonton, all the time I was in your automobile, I put on a martyred expression – like this – as if I was
bored to death with every luxury under the sun. I had the
time of my life.'

She sent her hat flying across the room, and her hair fell
tumbling over her forehead and cheeks. She perched herself on a rather high stool, and tucked her knees up under
her chin.

'Well, Tonton? You look as if you were dying of boredom. What about a game of piquet? It's Sunday, and

Mamma doesn't come back between the two performances. Who's been eating all my liquorice? Oh, Tonton, you can't get away with that! The least you can do is to send me some more to make up for it.'

'Gilberte, your manners!' scolded Madame Alvarez. 'Your knees! Gaston hasn't the time to bother about your liquorice. Pull down your skirts! Gaston, would you like me to send her to her room?'

Young Lachaille, with one eye on the dirty pack of cards in Gilberte's hand, was longing simultaneously to give way to tears, to confide his sorrows, to go to sleep in the old armchair, and to play piquet.

'Let the child stay! In this room I can relax. It's restful. Gigi, I'll play you for twenty pounds of sugar.'

'Your sugar's not very tempting. I much prefer sweets.'

'It's the same thing. And sugar is better for you than sweets.'

'You only say that because you make it.'

'Gilberte, you forget yourself!'

A smile enlivened the mournful eyes of Gaston Lachaille.

'Let her say what she likes, Mamita. And if I lose, Gigi, what would you like? A pair of silk stockings?'

The corners of Gilberte's big, childish mouth fell.

'Silk stockings make my legs itch. I would rather . . .'

She raised the snub-nosed face of an angel towards the ceiling, put her head on one side, and tossed her curls from one cheek to the other.

'I would rather have an eau-de-nil Persephone corset, with rococo roses embroidered on the suspenders. No. I'd rather have a music-case.'

'Are you studying music now?'

'No, but my older friends at school carry their copybooks in music-cases, because it makes them look like students at the Conservatoire.'

'Gilberte, you are making too free!' said Madame Alvarez.

'You shall have your case, and your liquorice. Cut, Gigi.'

The next moment, the heir of Lachaille-Sugar was deep in the game. His prominent nose, large enough to appear false, and his slightly negroid eyes did not in the least intimidate his opponent. With her elbows on the table, her shoulders on a level with her ears, and her blue eyes and red cheeks at their most vivid, she looked like a tipsy page. They both played passionately, almost in silence, exchanging occasional insults under their breath. 'You spindly spider! You sorrel run to seed!' Lachaille muttered. 'You old crow's beak!' the girl countered. The March twilight deepened over the narrow street.

'Please don't think I want you to go, Gaston,' said Madame Alvarez, 'but it's half-past seven. Will you excuse me while I just see about our dinner?'

'Half-past seven!' cried Lachaille, 'and I'm supposed to be dining at Larue with de Dion, Feydeau, and one of the Barthous! This must be the last hand, Gigi.'

'Why one of the Barthous?' asked Gilberte. 'Are there several of them?'

'Two. One handsome and the other less so. The best known is the least handsome.'

'That's not fair,' said Gilberte. 'And Feydeau, who's he?'

Lachaille plopped down his cards in amazement.

'Well, I declare! She doesn't know who Feydeau is! Don't you ever go to a play?'

'Hardly ever, Tonton.'

'Don't you like the theatre?'

'I'm not mad about it. And Grandmamma and Aunt Alicia both say that going to plays prevents one from thinking about the serious side of life. Don't tell Grandmamma I told you.'

She shifted the weight of her hair away from her ears, and let it fall forward again. 'Phew!' she sighed. 'This mane does make me hot!'

'And what do they mean by the serious side of life?'

'Oh, I don't know it all off by heart, Uncle Gaston. And, what's more, they don't always agree about it. Grandmamma says: "Don't read novels, they only depress you.

Don't put on powder, it ruins the complexion. Don't wear stays, they spoil the figure. Don't dawdle and gaze at shop windows when you're by yourself. Don't get to know the families of your school friends, especially not the fathers who wait at the gates to fetch their daughters home from school." '

She spoke very rapidly, panting between words like a child who has been running.

'And on top of that Aunt Alicia goes off on another tack! I've reached the age where I can wear stays, and I should take lessons in dancing and deportment, and I should be aware of what's going on, and know the meaning of "carat", and not be taken in by the clothes that actresses wear. "It's quite simple," she tells me. "Of all the dresses you see on the stage, nineteen out of twenty would look ridiculous in the paddock." In fact, my head is fit to split with it all! What shall you be eating at Larue this evening, Tonton?'

'How should I know! *Filets de sole aux moules*, for a change. And of course, saddle of lamb with truffles. Do get on with the game, Gigi! I've got a point of five.'

'That won't get you anywhere. I've got all the cards in the pack. Here, at home, we're having the warmed-up remains of the *cassoulet*. I'm very fond of *cassoulet*.'

'A plain dish of *cassoulet* with bacon rind,' said Inez Alvarez modestly, as she came in. 'Goose was exorbitant this week.'

'I'll have one sent to you from Bon-Abri,' said Gaston.

'Thank you very much, Gaston. Gigi, help Monsieur Lachaille on with his overcoat. Fetch him his hat and stick!'

When Lachaille had gone, rather sulky after a regretful sniff at the warmed up *cassoulet*, Madame Alvarez turned to her granddaughter.

'Will you please inform me, Gilberte, why it was you returned so early from Aunt Alicia's? I didn't ask you in front of Gaston. Family matters must never be discussed in front of a third person, remember that!'

'There's no mystery about it, Grandmamma. Aunt Alicia was wearing her little lace cap to show me she had a headache. She said to me, "I'm not very well." I said to her, "Oh, then I mustn't tire you out. I'll go home again." She said to me, "Sit down and rest for five minutes." "Oh!" I said to her, "I'm not tired. I drove here." "You drove here!" she said to me, raising her hands like this. As you may imagine, I had kept the motor-car waiting a few minutes, to show Aunt Alicia. "Yes," I said to her. "The four-seater de-Dion-Bouton-with-the-collapsible-hood, which Tonton lent me while he was paying a call on us. He has had a rumpus with Liane." "Who do you think you're talking to?" she says to me. "I've not yet got one foot in the grave! I'm still kept informed about public events when they're important. I know that he has had a rumpus with that great lamp-post of a woman. Well, you'd better run along home, and not bother about a poor ill old creature like me." She waved to me from the window as I got into the motor-car.'

Madame Alvarez pursed her lips.

'A poor ill old creature! She has never suffered so much as a cold in her life! I like that! What . . . ?'

'Grandmamma, do you think he'll remember my liquorice and the music-case?'

Madame Alvarez slowly lifted her heavy eyes towards the ceiling.

'Perhaps, my child, perhaps.'

'But, as he lost, he owes them to me, doesn't he?'

'Yes, yes, he owes them to you. Perhaps you'll get them after all. Slip on your pinafore, and set the table. Put away your cards.'

'Yes, Grandmamma. Grandmamma, what did he tell you about Madame Liane? Is it true she hopped it with Sandomir and the rope of pearls?'

'In the first place, one doesn't say "hopped it". In the second, come here and let me tighten your ribbon, so that your curls won't get soaked in the soup. And finally, the sayings and doings of a person who has broken the rules of etiquette are not for your ears. These happen to be Gaston's private affairs.'

'But, Grandmamma, they are no longer private, since everyone's talking about them, and the whole thing came out in *Gil Blas*.'

'Silence! All you need to know is that the conduct of Madame Liane d'Exelmans has been the reverse of sensible. The ham for your mother is between two plates: you will put it in the larder.'

Gilberte was asleep when her mother – Andrée Alvar, in small type on the Opéra-Comique play-bills – returned home. Madame Alvarez, the elder, seated at a game of patience, enquired from force of habit whether she was not too tired. Following polite family custom, Andrée reproached her mother for having waited up, and Madame Alvarez made her ritual reply.

'I shouldn't sleep in peace unless I knew you were in. There is some ham, and a little bowl of warm *cassoulet*. And some stewed prunes. The beer is on the window-sill.'

'The child is in bed?'

'Of course.'

Andrée Alvar made a solid meal – pessimists have good appetites. She still looked pretty in theatrical make-up. Without it, the rims of her eyes were pink and her lips colourless. For this reason, Aunt Alicia declared, Andrée never met with the admiration in real life that she gained on the stage.

'Did you sing well, my child?'

'Yes, I sang well. But where does it get me? All the applause goes to Tiphaine, as you may well imagine. Oh dear, oh dear, I really don't think I can bear to go on with this sort of life.'

'It was your own choice. But you would bear it much better,' said Madame Alvarez sententiously, 'if you had someone! It's your loneliness that gets on your nerves, and you take such black views. You're behaving contrary to nature.'

'Oh, Mother, don't start that all over again. I'm tired enough as it is. What news is there?'

'None. Everyone's talking of Gaston's break with Liane.'

'That's certainly the case: even in the green-room at the Opéra-Comique, which can hardly be called up-to-date.'

'It's an event of world-wide interest,' said Madame Alvarez.

'Is there any idea of who's in the running?'

'I should think not! It's far too recent. He is in full mourning, so to speak. Can you believe it, at a quarter to eight he was sitting exactly where you are now, playing a game of piquet with Gigi? He says he has no wish to attend the Battle of Flowers.'

'Not really!'

'Yes. If he doesn't go, it will cause a great deal of talk. I advised him to think twice before taking such a decision.'

'They were saying at the Théâtre that a certain music-hall artiste might stand a chance,' said Andrée. 'The one billed as the Cobra at the Olympia. It seems she does an acrobatic turn, and is brought on in a basket hardly big enough for a fox-terrier, and from this she uncurls like a snake.'

Madame Alvarez protruded her heavy lower lip in contempt.

'What an idea! Gaston Lachaille has not sunk to that level! A music-hall performer! Do him the justice to admit that, as befits a bachelor of his standing, he has always confined himself to the great ladies of the profession.'

'A fine pack of bitches!' murmured Andrée.

'Be more careful how you express yourself, my child. Calling people and things by their names has never done anyone any good. Gaston's mistresses have all had an air about them. A liaison with a great professional lady is the only suitable way for him to wait for a great marriage, always supposing that some day he does marry. Whatever may happen, we're in the front row when anything fresh turns up. Gaston has such confidence in me! I wish you had seen him asking me for camomile! A boy, a regular boy! Indeed, he is only thirty-three. And all that wealth weighs so heavily on his shoulders.'

Andrée's pink eyelids blinked ironically.

'Pity him, Mother, if you like. I'm not complaining, but all the time we've known Gaston, he has never given you anything except his confidence.'

'He owes us nothing. And thanks to him we've always had sugar for our jams, and, from time to time, for my *curaçao*; and birds from his farm, and odds and ends for the child.'

'If you're satisfied with that!'

Madame Alvarez held high her majestic head.

'Perfectly satisfied. And even if I was not, what difference would it make?'

'In fact, as far as we're concerned, Gaston Lachaille, rich as he is, behaves as if he wasn't rich at all. Supposing we were in real straits! Would he come to our rescue, do you suppose?'

Madame Alvarez placed her hand on her heart.

'I'm convinced that he would,' she said. And after a pause, she added, 'But I would rather not have to ask him.'

Andrée picked up the *Journal* again, in which there was a photograph of Liane the ex-mistress. 'When you take a good look at her, she's not so extraordinary.'

'You're wrong,' retorted Madame Alvarez. 'She is extraordinary. Otherwise she would not be so famous. Success and celebrity are not a matter of luck. You talk like those scatterbrains who say, "Seven rows of pearls would look every bit as well on me as on Madame de Pougy. She certainly cuts a dash – but so could I." Such nonsense makes me laugh. Take what's left of the camomile to bathe your eyes.'

'Thank you, Mother. Did the child go to Aunt Alicia's?'

'She did indeed, and in Gaston's motor-car, what's more! He lent it to her. It can go at forty miles an hour, I believe! She was in the seventh heaven.'

'Poor lamb, I wonder what she'll make of her life. She's

quite capable of ending up as a mannequin or a sales-
woman. She's so backward. At her age, I –'

There was no indulgence in the glance Madame Alvarez
bestowed on her daughter.

'Don't boast too much about what you were doing when
you were her age. If I remember rightly, at her age you
were snapping your fingers at Monsieur Mennesson and all
his flour-mills, though he was perfectly ready to make you
your fortune. Instead, you must needs bolt with a wretched
music-master.'

Andrée Alvar kissed her mother's lustrous plaits.

'My darling Mother, don't curse me at this hour. I'm so
sleepy. Good night, Mother. I've a rehearsal tomorrow at
a quarter to one. I'll eat at the tea-shop during the interval;
don't bother about me.'

She yawned and walked in the dark through the little
room where her daughter was asleep. All she could see of
Gilberte in the obscurity was a brush of hair and the
Russian braid of her nightdress. She locked herself into
the exiguous bathroom and, late though it was, lit the
gas under a kettle. Madame Alvarez had instilled into her
progeny, among other virtues, a respect for certain rites.
One of her maxims was, 'You can, at a pinch, leave the
face till the morning, when travelling or pressed for time.
For a woman, attention to the lower parts is the first law of
self-respect.'

The last to go to bed, Madame Alvarez was the first to
rise, and allowed the daily woman no hand in preparing
the breakfast coffee. She slept in the dining-sitting-room,
on a divan-bed, and, at the stroke of half-past seven, she
opened the door to the papers, the quart of milk, and the
daily woman – who was carrying the others. By eight
o'clock she had taken out her curling-pins, and her beautiful coils were dressed and smooth. At ten minutes to nine
Gilberte left for school, clean and tidy, her hair well-
brushed. At ten o'clock Madame Alvarez was 'thinking
about' the midday meal, that is, she got into her mackin-

tosh, slipped her arm through the handle of her shopping net, and set off to market.

On that day, as on all other days, she made sure that her granddaughter would not be late; she placed the coffee-pot and the jug of milk piping hot on the table, and un-folded the newspaper while waiting for her. Gilberte came in fresh as a flower, smelling of lavender-water, with some vestiges of sleep still clinging to her. A cry from Madame Alvarez made her fully wide awake.

'Call your mother, Gigi! Liane d'Exelmans has com-mitted suicide.'

The child replied with a long drawn-out 'Oooh!' and asked, 'Is she dead?'

'Of course not. She knows what she's about.'

'How did she do it, Grandmamma? A revolver?'

Madame Alvarez looked pityingly at her granddaughter.

'The idea! Laudanum, as usual. "*Doctors Morèze and Pelledoux, who have never left the heart-broken beauty's bedside, cannot yet answer for her life, but their diagnosis is reassuring* ..." My own diagnosis is that if Madame d'Exelmans goes on playing that game, she'll end by ruin-ing her stomach.'

'The last time she killed herself, Grandmamma, was for the sake of Prince Georgevitch, wasn't it?'

'Where are your brains, my darling? It was for Count Berthou de Sauveterre.'

'Oh, so it was. And what will Tonton do now, do you think?'

A dreamy look passed across the huge eyes of Madame Alvarez.

'It's a toss-up, my child. We shall know everything in good time, even if he starts by refusing to give an inter-view to anybody. You must always start by refusing to give an interview to anybody. Then later you can fill the front page. Tell the concierge, by the way, to get us the evening papers. Have you had enough to eat? Did you have your second cup of milk, and your two pieces of bread and butter? Put on your gloves before you go out. Don't dawdle on the way. I'm going to call your mother. What a story! Andrée, are you asleep? Oh, so you're out of bed! Andrée, Liane has committed suicide!'

'That's a nice change!' muttered Andrée. 'She's only the one idea in her head, that woman, but she sticks to it.'

'You've not taken out your curlers yet, Andrée?'

'And have my hair go limp in the middle of rehearsal? No thank you!'

Madame Alvarez ran her eyes over her daughter, from the spiky tips of her curlers to the felt slippers. 'It's plain that there's no man here for you to bother about, my child! A man in the house soon cures a woman of traipsing about in dressing-gown and slippers. What an excitement, this suicide! Unsuccessful, of course.'

Andrée's pallid lips parted in a contemptuous smile: 'It's getting too boring – the way she takes laudanum as if it was castor oil!'

'Anyhow, who cares about her? It's the Lachaille heir who matters. This is the first time such a thing has happened to him. He's already had, let me see. He's had Gentiane, who stole certain papers; then that foreigner, who tried to force him into marriage; but Liane is his first suicide. In such circumstances, a man so much in the public eye has to be extremely careful about what line he takes.'

'Him! He'll be bursting with pride, you may be sure.'

'And with good reason, too,' said Madame Alvarez. 'We shall be seeing great things before very long. I wonder what Alicia will have to say about the situation.'

'She'll do her best to make a mountain out of a molehill.'

'Alicia is no angel. But I must confess that she is far-sighted. And that without ever leaving her room!'

'She's no need to, since she has the telephone. Mother, won't you have one put in here?'

'It's expensive,' said Madame Alvarez, thoughtfully. 'We only just manage to make both ends meet, as it is. The telephone is of real use only to important businessmen, or to women who have something to hide. Now, if you were to change your mode of life – and I'm only putting it forward as a supposition – and if Gigi were to start on a life of her own, I should be the first to say, "We'll have the telephone put in." But we haven't reached that point yet, unfortunately.'

She allowed herself a single sigh, pulled on her rubber gloves, and coolly set about her household chores. Thanks to her care, the oldest flat was growing old without too many signs of deterioration. She retained, from her past life, the honourable habits of women who have lost their honour, and these she taught to her daughter and her daughter's daughter. Sheets never stayed on the beds longer than ten days, and the char-cum-washerwoman told everyone that the chemises and drawers of the ladies of Madame Alvarez' household were changed more often than she could count, and so were the table napkins. At any moment, at the cry of 'Gigi, take off your shoes!' Gilberte had to remove shoes and stockings, exhibit white feet to the closest inspection, and announce the least suspicion of a corn.

During the week following Madame d'Exelman's suicide, Lachaille's reactions were somewhat incoherent. He engaged the stars of the National Musical Academy to dance at a midnight fête held at his own house, and, wishing to give a supper party at the Pré-Catalan, he arranged for that restaurant to open a fortnight earlier than was their custom. The clowns, Footit et Chocolat, did a turn: Rita del Erido caracoled on horseback between the supper tables, wearing a divided skirt of white lace flounces, a white hat on her black hair with white ostrich feathers frothing round the relentless beauty of her face. Indeed, Paris mistakenly proclaimed, such was her beauty, that Gaston Lachaille was about to hoist her (astride) upon a throne of sugar. Twenty-four hours later, Paris remedied the mistake. For, owing to the false prophecies it had published, *Gil Blas* nearly lost the subsidy it received from Gaston Lachaille. A specialized weekly, *Paris en amour*, provided another red herring, under the headline: '*Young*

Yankee millionairess makes no secret of weakness for French sugar'.

Madame Alvarez' ample bust shook with incredulous laughter when she read the daily papers: she had received her information from none other than Gaston Lachaille in person. Twice in ten days, he had found time to drop in for a cup of camomile, to sink into the depths of the now sagging conch-shaped armchair, and there forget his business worries and his dislike of being unattached. He even brought Gigi an absurd Russian leather music-case with a silver-gilt clasp, and twenty boxes of liquorice. Madame Alvarez was given a *pâté de foie gras* and six bottles of champagne, and of these bounties Tonton Lachaille partook by inviting himself to dinner. Throughout the meal, Gilberte regaled them rather tipsily with tittle-tattle about her school, and later won Gaston's gold pencil at piquet. He lost with good grace, recovered his spirits, laughed and, pointing to the child, said to Madame Alvarez, 'There's my best pal!' Madame Alvarez' Spanish eyes moved with slow watchfulness from Gigi's reddened cheeks and white teeth to Lachaille, who was pulling her hair by the fistful. 'You little devil, you'd the fourth king up your sleeve all the time!'

It was at this moment that Andrée, returning from the Opéra-Comique, looked at Gigi's dishevelled head rolling against Lachaille's sleeve and saw the tears of excited laughter in her lovely slate-blue eyes. She said nothing, and accepted a glass of champagne, then another, and yet another. After her third glass, Gaston Lachaille was threatened with the Bell Song from *Lakmé,* at which point her mother led her away to bed.

The following day, no one spoke of this family party except Gilberte, who exclaimed, 'Never, never in all my life, have I laughed so much! And the pencil-case is real gold!' Her unreserved chatter met with a strange silence, or rather with 'Now then, Gigi, try to be a little more serious!' thrown out almost absent-mindedly.

After that, Gaston Lachaille let a fortnight go by without giving any sign of life, and the Alvarez family gathered its information from the papers only.

'Did you see, Andrée? In the Gossip Column it says that Monsieur Gaston Lachaille has left for Monte Carlo. *The reason for this seems to be of a sentimental nature – a secret that we respect*. What next!'

'Would you believe it, Grandmamma. Lydia Poret was saying at the dancing class that Liane travelled on the same train as Tonton, but in another compartment! Grandmamma, do you think it can be true?'

Madame Alvarez shrugged her shoulders.

'If it was true, how on earth would those Porets know? Have they become friends with Monsieur Lachaille all of a sudden?'

'No, but Lydia Poret heard the story in her aunt's dressing-room at the Comédie Française.'

Madame Alvarez exchanged looks with her daughter.

'In her dressing-room! That explains everything!' she exclaimed, for she held the theatrical profession in contempt, although Andrée worked so hard. When Madame Émilienne d'Alençon had decided to present performing rabbits, and Madame de Pougy – shyer on the stage than any young girl – had amused herself by miming the part of Columbine in spangled black tulle, Madame Alvarez had stigmatized them both in a single phrase. 'What! have they sunk to that?'

'Grandmamma, tell me, Grandmamma, do you know him, this Prince Radziwill?' Gilberte went on again.

'What's come over the child today? Has she been bitten by a flea? Which Prince Radziwill, to begin with? There's more than one.'

'I don't know,' said Gigi. 'The one who's getting married. Among the list of presents, it says here, *"are three writing-sets in malachite"*. What is malachite?'

'Oh, you're being tiresome, child. If he's getting married, he's no longer interesting.'

'But if Tonton got married, wouldn't he be interesting either?'

'It all depends. It would be interesting if he were to marry his mistress. When Prince Cheniaguine married Valérie d'Aigreville, it was obvious that the life she had led for him for the past fifteen years was all he wanted; scenes, plates flung across the room, and reconciliations in the middle of the Restaurant Durand, Place de la Madeleine. Clearly, she was a woman who knew how to make herself valued. But all that is too complicated for you, my poor Gigi.'

'And do you think it's to marry Liane that they've gone away together?'

Madame Alvarez pressed her forehead against the window-pane, and seemed to be consulting the spring sunshine, which bestowed upon the street a bright side and a shady one.

'No,' she said, 'not if I know anything about anything. I must have a word with Alicia. Gigi, come with me as far as her house; you can leave me there and find your way back along the quais. It will give you some fresh air, since, it would seem, one must have fresh air nowadays. I have never been in the habit of taking the air more than twice a year, myself, at Cabourg and at Monte Carlo. And I am none the worse for that.'

That evening Madame Alvarez came in so late that the family dined off tepid soup, cold meat, and some cakes sent round by Aunt Alicia. To Gilberte's 'Well, what did she have to say?' she presented an icy front, and replied in clarion tones:

'She says she is going to teach you how to eat ortolans.'

'Scrumptious!' cried Gilberte. 'And what did she say about the summer frock she promised me?'

'She said she would see. And that's no reason why you should be displeased with the result.'

'Oh!' said Gilberte gloomily.

'She also wants you to go to luncheon with her on Thursday, sharp at twelve.'

'With you, too, Grandmamma?'

Madame Alvarez looked at the willowy slip of a girl

facing her across the table, at her high, rosy cheekbones beneath eyes as blue as an evening sky, at her strong even teeth biting a fresh-coloured but slightly chapped lip, and at the primitive splendour of her ash-gold hair.

'No,' she said at last. 'Without me.'

Gilberte got up and wound an arm about her grandmother's neck.

'The way you said that, Grandmamma, surely doesn't mean that your going to send me to live with Aunt Alicia? I don't want to leave here, Grandmamma!'

Madame Alvarez cleared her throat, gave a little cough and smiled.

'Goodness gracious, what a foolish creature you are! Leave here! Why, my poor Gigi, I'm not scolding you, but you've not reached the first stage towards leaving.'

For a bell-pull, Aunt Alicia had hung from her front door a length of bead-embroidered braid on a background of twining green vine-leaves and purple grapes. The door itself, varnished and revarnished till it glistened, shone with the glow of a dark-brown caramel. From the very threshold, where she was admitted by a 'man-servant', Gilberte enjoyed in her undiscriminating way an atmosphere of discreet luxury. The carpet, spread with Persian rugs, seemed to lend her wings. After hearing Madame Alvarez pronounce her sister's Louis XV little drawing-room to be 'boredom itself', Gilberte echoed her words by saying: 'Aunt Alicia's drawing-room is very pretty, but it's boredom itself!' reserving her admiration for the dining room, furnished in pale almost golden lemon wood dating from the Directoire, quite plain but for the grain of a wood as transparent as wax. 'I shall buy myself a set like that one day,' Gigi had once said in all innocence.

'In the Faubourg Antoine, I dare say,' Aunt Alicia had answered teasingly, with a smile of her cupid's bow mouth and a flash of small teeth.

She was seventy years old. Her fastidious taste was everywhere apparent; in her silver-grey bedroom with its red

Chinese vases, in her narrow white bathroom as warm as a
hot-house, and in her robust health, concealed by a pre-
tence of delicacy. The men of her generation, when trying
to describe Alicia de Saint-Efflam, fumbled for words and
could only exclaim, 'Oh, my dear fellow!' or 'Nothing
could give you the faintest ideah!' Those who had known
her intimately produced photographs which younger men
found ordinary enough. 'Was she really so lovely? You
wouldn't think so from her photographs!' Looking at
portraits of her, old admirers would pause for an instant,
recollecting the turn of a wrist like a swan's neck, the tiny
ear, the profile revealing a delicious kinship between the
heart-shaped mouth and the wide-cut eyelids with their
long lashes.

Gilberte kissed the pretty old lady, who was wearing a
peak of black Chantilly lace on her white hair, and, on her
slightly dumpy figure, a tea-gown of shot taffeta.

'You have one of your headaches, Aunt Alicia?'

'I'm not sure yet,' replied Aunt Alicia; 'it depends on the
luncheon. Come quickly; the eggs are ready! Take off your
coat! What on earth is that dress?'

'One of Mamma's, altered to fit me. Are they difficult
eggs today?'

'Not at all. *Œufs brouillés aux croutons.* The ortolans
are not difficult, either. And you shall have chocolate
cream. So shall I.'

With her young voice, a touch of pink on her amiable
wrinkles, and lace on her white hair. Aunt Alicia was the
perfect stage marquise. Gilberte had the greatest reverence
for her aunt. In sitting down to table in her presence, she
would pull her skirt up behind, join her knees, hold her
elbows close to her sides, straighten her shoulder-blades,
and to all appearances become the perfect young lady. She
would remember what she had been taught, break her
bread quietly, eat with her mouth shut, and take care,
when cutting her meat, not to let her forefinger reach the
blade of her knife.

Today her hair, severely tied back in a heavy knot at

the nape of her neck, disclosed the fresh line of her forehead and ears, and a very powerful throat, rising from the
rather ill-cut opening of her altered dress. This was a dingy
blue, the bodice pleated about a let-in piece and, to cheer
up this patchwork, three rows of mohair braid had been
sewn round the hem of the skirt, and three times three rows
of mohair braid round the sleeves, between the wrist and
the elbow.

Aunt Alicia, sitting opposite her niece and examining
her through fine dark eyes, could find no fault.

'How old are you?' she asked suddenly.

'The same as I was the other day, Aunt. Fifteen and a
half. Aunt, what do you really think of this business of
Tonton Gaston?'

'Why? Does it interest you?'

'Of course, Aunt. It worries me. If Tonton takes up with
another lady, he won't come and play piquet with us any
more or drink camomile tea – at least not for some time.
That would be a shame.'

'That's one way of looking at it, certainly.'

Aunt Alicia examined her niece critically, through
narrowed eyelids.

'Do you work hard, in class? Who are your friends?
Ortolans should be cut in two, with one quick stroke of
the knife, and no grating of the blade on the plate. Bite
up each half. The bones don't matter. Go on eating while
you answer my question, but don't talk with your mouth
full. You must manage it. If I can, you can. What friends
have you made?'

'None, Aunt. Grandmamma won't even let me have tea
with the families of my school friends.'

'She is quite right. Apart from that, there is no one who
follows you, no little clerk hanging round your skirts? No
schoolboy? No older man? I warn you, I shall know at
once if you lie to me.'

Gilberte gazed at the bright face of the imperious old
lady who was questioning her so sharply.

'Why, no, Aunt, no one. Has somebody been telling you

tales about me? I am always on my own. And why does Grandmamma stop me from accepting invitations?'

'She is right, for once. You would only be invited by ordinary people – that is to say, useless people.'

'And what about us? Aren't we ordinary people ourselves?'

'No.'

'What makes these ordinary people inferior to us?'

'They have weak heads and dissolute bodies. Besides, they are married. But I don't think you understand.'

'Yes, Aunt, I understand that we don't marry.'

'Marriage is not forbidden to us. Instead of marrying "at once", it sometimes happens that we marry "at last".'

'But does that prevent me from seeing girls of my own age?'

'Yes. Are you bored at home? Well, be a little bored. It's not a bad thing. Boredom helps one to make decisions. What is the matter? Tears? The tears of a silly child who is backward for her age. Have another ortolan.'

Aunt Alicia, with three glittering fingers, grasped the stem of her glass and raised it in a toast.

'To you and me, Gigi! You shall have an Egyptian cigarette with your coffee. On condition that you do not make the end of it wet, and that you don't spit out specks of tobacco – going *ptu, ptu.* I shall also give you a note to the *première vendeuse* at Béchoff-David, an old friend of mine who was not a success. Your wardrobe is going to be changed. Nothing venture, nothing have.'

The dark-blue eyes gleamed. Gilberte stammered with joy.

'Aunt! Aunt! I'm going to . . . to Bé –'

'– choff-David. But I thought you weren't interested in clothes?'

Gilberte blushed.

'Aunt, I'm not interested in home-made clothes.'

'I sympathize with you. Can it be that you have taste? When you think of looking your best, how do you see yourself dressed?'

'Oh, but I know just what would suit me, Aunt! I've seen –'

'Explain yourself without gestures. The moment you gesticulate you look common.'

'I've seen a dress . . . oh, a dress created for Madame Lucy Gérard! Myriads of tiny ruffles of pearl-grey silk muslin from top to bottom. And then a dress of lavender-blue cloth cut out on a black velvet foundation, the cut-out design making a sort of peacock's tail on the train.'

The small hand with its precious stones flashed through the air.

'Enough! Enough! I see your fancy is to be dressed like a leading *comédienne* at the Théâtre Français – and don't take that as a compliment! Come and pour out the coffee. And without jerking up the lip of the coffee-pot to prevent the drop from falling. I'd rather have a foot-bath in my saucer than see you juggling like a waiter in a café.'

The next hour passed very quickly for Gilberte: Aunt Alicia had unlocked her casket of jewels to use for a lesson that dazzled her.

'What is that, Gigi?'

'A marquise diamond.'

'We say, a marquise-shaped brilliant. And that?'

'A topaz.'

Aunt Alicia threw up her hands and the sunlight, glancing off her rings, set off a myriad scintillations.

'A topaz! I have suffered many humiliations, but this surpasses them all. A topaz among my jewels! Why not an aquamarine or a chrysolite? It's a jonquil diamond, little goose, and you won't often see its like. And this?'

Gilberte half-opened her mouth, as though in a dream.

'Oh! That's an emerald. Oh, how beautiful it is!'

Aunt Alicia slipped the large square-cut emerald on one of her thin fingers and was lost in silence.

'Do you see,' she said in a hushed voice, 'that almost blue flame darting about in the depths of the green light? Only the most beautiful emeralds contain that miracle of elusive blue.'

'Who gave it to you, Aunt?' Gilberte dared to ask.

'A king,' said Aunt Alicia simply.

'A great king?'

'No. A little one. Great kings do not give very fine stones.'

'Why not?'

For a fleeting moment, Aunt Alicia proffered a glimpse of her tiny white teeth.

'If you want my opinion, it's because they don't want to. Between ourselves, the little ones don't either.'

'Then who does give great big stones?'

'Who? The shy. The proud, too. And the bounders, because they think that to give a monster jewel is a sign of good breeding. Sometimes a woman does, to humiliate a man. Never wear second-rate jewels; wait till the really good ones come to you.'

'And if they don't?'

'Well, then it can't be helped. Rather than a wretched hundred-guinea diamond, wear a half-crown ring. In that case you can say, "It's a memento. I never part with it, day or night." Don't ever wear artistic jewellery; it wrecks a woman's reputation."

'What is an artistic jewel?'

'It all depends. A mermaid in gold, with eyes of chryso-prase. An Egyptian scarab. A large engraved amethyst. A not very heavy bracelet said to have been chased by a master-hand. A lyre or star, mounted as a brooch. A studded tortoise. In a word, all of them frightful. Never wear baroque pearls, not even as hat-pins. Beware above all things, of family jewels!'

'But Grandmamma has a beautiful cameo, set as a medallion.'

'There are no beautiful cameos,' said Aunt Alicia with a toss of the head. 'There are precious stones and pearls. There are white, yellow, blue, blue-white, or pink diamonds. We won't speak of black diamonds, they're not worth mentioning. Then there are rubies – when you can be sure of them; sapphires, when they come from Kashmir;

emeralds, provided they have no fatal flaw, or are not too light in colour, or have a yellowish tint.'

'Aunt, I am very fond of opals, too.'

'I am very sorry, but you are not to wear them. I won't allow it.'

Dumbfounded, Gilberte remained for a moment open-mouthed.

'Oh! Do you too, Aunt, really believe that they bring bad luck?'

'Why in the world not? You silly little creature,' Alicia went bubbling on, 'you must pretend to believe in such things. Believe in opals, believe – let's see, what can I suggest – in turquoises that die, in the evil eye . . .'

'But,' said Gigi, haltingly, 'those are . . . are superstitions!'

'Of course they are, child. They also go by the name of weaknesses. A pretty little collection of weaknesses and a terror of spiders are our indispensable stock-in-trade with the men.'

'Why, Aunt?'

The old lady closed the casket, and kept Gilberte kneeling before her.

'Because nine men out of ten are superstitious, nineteen out of twenty believe in the evil eye, and ninety eight out of a hundred are afraid of spiders. They forgive us – oh! for many things, but not for the absence in us of their own feelings. What makes you sigh?'

'I shall never remember all that!'

'The important thing is not for you to remember, but for me to know it.'

'Aunt, what is a writing-set in . . . in malachite?'

'Always a calamity. But where on earth did you pick up such terms?'

'From the list of presents at grand weddings, Aunt, printed in the papers.'

'Nice reading! But, at least you can gather from it what kind of presents you should never give or accept.'

While speaking, she began to touch here and there the young face on a level with her own, with the sharp pointed nail of her index finger. She lifted one slightly chapped lip, inspected the spotless enamel of the teeth.

'A fine jaw, my girl! With such teeth, I should have gobbled up Paris, and the rest of the world into the bargain. As it was, I had a good bite out of it. What's this you've got here? A small pimple? You shouldn't have a small pimple near your nose. And this? You've squeezed a blackhead. You've no business to have such things, or to squeeze them. I'll give you some of my astringent lotion. You mustn't eat anything from the pork-butchers' except cooked ham. You don't put on powder?'

'Grandmamma won't let me.'

'I should hope not. . . . Let me smell your breath. Not that it means anything at this hour, you've just had luncheon.'

She laid her hands on Gigi's shoulders.

'Pay attention to what I'm going to say. You have it in your power to please. You have an impossible little nose, a nondescript mouth, cheeks rather like the wife of a *moujik –*'

'Oh, Aunt!' sighed Gilberte.

'But, with your eyes and eyelashes, your teeth, and your hair, you can get away with it, if you're not a perfect fool. As for the rest –'

She cupped her hands like conch-shells over Gigi's bosom and smiled.

'A promise, but a pretty promise, neatly moulded. Don't eat too many almonds; they add weight to the breasts. Ah! remind me to teach you how to choose cigars.'

Gilberte opened her eyes so wide that the tips of her lashes touched her eyebrows.

'Why?'

She received a little tap on the cheek.

'Because – because I do nothing without good reason. If I take you in hand at all, I must do it thoroughly. Once a woman understands the tastes of a man, cigars included, and once a man knows what pleases a woman, they may be said to be well matched.'

'And then they fight,' concluded Gigi with a knowing air.

'What do you mean, they fight?'

The old lady looked at Gigi in consternation.

'Ah!' she added, 'you certainly never invented the triple mirror! Come, you little psychologist! Let me give you a note for Madame Henriette at Béchoff.'

While her aunt was writing at a miniature rose-pink escritoire, Gilberte breathed in the scent of the fastidiously furnished room. Without wanting them for herself, she examined the objects she knew so well but hardly appreciated: Cupid, the Archer, pointing to the hours on the mantelpiece; two rather daring pictures; a bed like the basin of a fountain and its chinchilla coverlet; a rosary of small seed pearls and the New Testament on the bedside table; two red Chinese vases fitted as lamps – a happy note against the grey of the walls.

'Run along, my little one. I shall send for you again quite soon. Don't forget to ask Victor for the cake you're to take home. Gently, don't disarrange my hair! And remember, I shall have my eye on you as you leave the house. Woe betide you if you march like a guardsman, or drag your feet behind you!'

The month of May fetched Gaston Lachaille back to Paris, and brought to Gilberte two well-cut dresses and a light-weight coat – 'a sack-coat like Cléo de Mérode's' she called it – as well as hats and boots and shoes. To these she added, on her own account, a few curls over the forehead, which cheapened her appearance. She paraded in front of Gaston in a blue-and-white dress reaching almost to the ground. 'A full seven and a half yards round, Tonton, my skirt measures!' She was more than proud of her slender waist, held in by a grosgrain sash with a silver buckle; but she tried every dodge to free her lovely strong neck from its whale-bone collar of 'imitation Venetian point' which matched the tucks of her bodice. The full sleeves and wide-flounced skirt of blue-and-white striped silk rustled deliciously, and Gilberte delighted in pecking at her sleeves, to puff them out just below the shoulder.

'You remind me of a performing monkey,' Lachaille said to her. 'I liked you much better in your old tartan dress. In that uncomfortable collar you look just like a hen with a full crop. Take a peep at yourself!'

Feeling a little ruffled, Gilberte turned round to face the looking-glass. She had a lump in one of her cheeks caused by a large caramel, out of a box sent all the way from Nice at Gaston's order.

'I've heard a good deal about you, Tonton,' she retorted, 'but I've never heard it said that you had any taste in clothes.'

He stared, almost choking, at this newly-fledged young woman, then turned to Madame Alvarez.

'Charming manners you've taught her! I congratulate you!'

Whereupon he left the house without drinking his camomile tea, and Madame Alvarez wrung her hands.

'Look what you've done for us now, my poor Gigi!'

'I know,' said Gigi, 'but then why does he go for me? He must know by now, I should think, that I can give as good as I get!'

Her grandmother shook her by the arm.

'But think what you've done, you wretched child! Good heavens! when will you learn to think? You've mortally offended the man, as likely as not. Just when we are doing our utmost to –'

'To do what, Grandmamma?'

'Why! to do everything to make an elegant young lady of you, to show you off to advantage.'

'For whose benefit, Grandmamma? You must admit that one doesn't have to turn oneself inside out for an old friend like Tonton!'

But Madame Alvarez admitted nothing: not even to her astonishment, when, the following day, Gaston Lachaille arrived in the best of spirits, wearing a light-coloured suit.

'Put on your hat, Gigi! I'm taking you out to tea.'

'Where?' cried Gigi.

'To the *Réservoirs*, at Versailles!'

'Hurrah!! Hurrah! Hurrah!' chanted Gilberte.

She turned towards the kitchen.

'Grandmamma, I'm having tea at the *Réservoirs*, with Tonton!'

Madame Alvarez appeared, and without stopping to untie the flowered satinette apron across her stomach, interposed her soft hand between Gilberte's arm and that of Gaston Lachaille.

'No, Gaston,' she said simply.

'What do you mean, No?'

'Oh, Grandmamma!' wailed Gigi.

Madame Alvarez seemed not to hear her.

'Go to your room a minute, Gigi! I should like to talk to Monsieur Lachaille in private.'

She watched Gilberte leave the room and close the door behind her; then, returning to Gaston, she met his dark rather brutal stare without flinching.

'What is the meaning of all this, Mamita? Ever since yesterday, I find quite a change here. What's going on?'

'I shall be glad if you will sit down, Gaston. I'm tired,' said Madame Alvarez. 'Oh, my poor legs!'

She sighed, waited for a response that did not come, and then untied her apron, under which she was wearing a black dress with a large cameo pinned upon it. She motioned her guest to a high-backed chair, keeping the armchair for herself. Then she sat down heavily, smoothed her greying black coils, and folded her hands on her lap. The unhurried movement of her large, dark, lambent eyes, and the ease with which she remained motionless, were sure signs of her self-control.

'Gaston, you cannot doubt my friendship for you.' Lachaille emitted a short, businesslike laugh, and tugged at his moustache. 'My friendship and my gratitude. Nevertheless, I must never forget that I have a soul entrusted to my care. Andrée, as you know, has neither the time nor the inclination to look after the girl. Our Gilberte has not got the gumption to make her own way in the world, like so many. She is just a child.'

'Of sixteen,' said Lachaille.

'Of nearly sixteen,' consented Madame Alvarez. 'For years you have been giving her sweets and playthings. She swears by Tonton, and by him alone. And now you want to take her out to tea, in your automobile, to the *Réservoirs!*'

Madame Alvarez placed a hand on her heart.

'Upon my soul and conscience, Gaston, if there were only you and me, I should say to you, "Take Gilberte anywhere you like, I entrust her to you blindly." But there are always the others. The eyes of the world are on you. To be seen *tête-à-tête* with you, is, for a woman –'

Gaston Lachaille lost patience.

'All right, all right. I understand. You want me to believe that once she is seen having tea with me, Gilberte is compromised! A slip of a girl, a flapper, a chit whom no one notices!'

'Let us say, rather,' interrupted Madame Alvarez gently, 'that she will be labelled. No matter where you put in an appearance, Gaston, your presence is remarked upon. A young girl who goes out alone with you is no longer an ordinary girl, or even – to put it bluntly – a respectable girl. Now our little Gilberte must not, above all things, cease to be an ordinary young girl, at least not by that method. So far as it concerns you, it will simply end in one more story to be added to the long list already in existence, but personally, when I read of it in *Gil Blas*, I shall not be amused.'

Gaston Lachaille rose, paced from the table to the door, then from the door to the window, before replying.

'Very good, Mamita, I have no wish to vex you. I shan't argue,' he said coldly. 'Keep your precious child.'

He turned round again to face Madame Alvarez, his chin held high.

'I can't help wondering, as a matter of interest, whom you are keeping her for! A clerk earning a hundred a year, who'll marry her and give her four children in three years?'

'I know the duty of a mother better than that,' said Madame Alvarez composedly. 'I shall do my best to entrust Gigi only to the care of a man capable of saying, "I take charge of her and answer for her future." May I have the pleasure of brewing you some camomile tea, Gaston?'

'No, thank you, I'm late already.'

'Would you like Gigi to come and say goodbye?'

'Don't bother. I'll see her another time. I can't say when, I'm sure. I'm very much taken up these days.'

'Never mind, Gaston; don't worry about her. Have a good time, Gaston.'

Once alone, Madame Alvarez mopped her forehead. and went to open the door of Gilberte's room.

'You were listening at the door, Gigi!'

'No, Grandmamma.'

'Yes, you had your ear to the key-hole. You must never listen at key-holes. You don't hear properly and so you get things all wrong. Monsieur Lachaille has gone.'

'So I can see,' said Gilberte.

'Now you must rub the new potatoes in a cloth; I'll sauté them when I come in.'

'Are you going out, Grandmamma?'

'I'm going round to see Alicia.'

'Again?'

'Is it your place to object?' said Madame Alvarez severely. 'You had better bathe your eyes in cold water, since you have been silly enough to cry.'

'Grandmamma!'

'What?'

'What difference could it make to you, if you'd let me go out with Tonton Gaston in my new dress?'

'Silence! If you can't understand anything about anything, at least let those who are capable of using their reason do so for you. And put on my rubber gloves before you touch the potatoes!'

Throughout the whole of the following week, silence

reigned over the Alvarez household, except for a surprise visit, one day, from Aunt Alicia. She arrived in a hired brougham, all black lace and dull silk with a rose at her shoulder, and carried on an anxious conversation, strictly between themselves, with her younger sister. As she was leaving, she bestowed only a moment's attention on Gilberte, pecked at her cheek with a fleeting kiss, and was gone.

'What did she want?' Gilberte asked Madame Alvarez.

'Oh, nothing . . . the address of the heart specialist who treated Madame Buffetery.'

Gilberte reflected for a moment.

'It was a lengthy one,' she said.

'What was lengthy?'

'The address of the heart specialist. Grandmamma, I should like a *cachet*. I have a headache.'

'But you had one yesterday. A headache doesn't last forty-eight hours!'

'Presumably my headaches are different from other people's,' said Gilberte, offended.

She was losing some of her sweetness, and, on her return from school, would make some such remark as 'My teacher has got his knife into me!' or complain of not being able to sleep. She was gradually slipping into a state of idleness, which her grandmother noticed, but did nothing to overcome.

One day Gigi was busy applying liquid chalk to her white canvas button boots, when Gaston Lachaille put in an appearance without ringing the bell. His hair was too long, his complexion sun-tanned, and he was wearing a broad check summer suit. He stopped short in front of Gilberte, who was perched high on a kitchen stool, her left hand shod with a boot.

'Oh! Grandmamma left the key in the door. That's just like her!'

As Gaston Lachaille looked at her without saying a word, she began to blush, put down the boot on the table and pulled her skirt down over her knees.

'So, Tonton, you slip in like a burglar! I believe you're thinner. Aren't you fed properly by that famous chef of yours who used to be with the Prince of Wales? Being thinner makes your eyes look larger, and at the same time makes your nose longer, and –'

'I have something to say to your grandmother,' interrupted Gaston Lachaille. 'Run into you room, Gigi!'

For a moment she remained open-mouthed; then she jumped off her stool. The strong column of her neck, like an archangel's, swelled with anger as she advanced upon Lachaille.

'Run into your room! Run into your room! And suppose I said the same to you? Who do you think you are here, ordering me to run into my room? All right, I'm going to my room! And I can tell you one thing; so long as you're in the house, I shan't come out of it!'

She slammed the door behind her, and there was a dramatic click of the bolt.

'Gaston,' breathed Madame Alvarez. 'I shall insist on the child apologizing. Yes, I shall insist. If necessary, I'll ...'

Gaston was not listening to her, and stood staring at the closed door.

'Now, Mamita,' said he, 'let us talk briefly and to the point.'

'Let us go over it all once again,' said Aunt Alicia. 'To begin with, you are quite sure he said, "She shall be spoiled, more than –" '

'Than any woman before her!'

'Yes, but that's the sort of vague phrase that every man comes out with. I like things cut and dried.'

'Just what they were, Alicia, for he said that he would guarantee Gigi against every imaginable mishap, even against himself, by an insurance policy; and that he regarded himself more or less as her godfather.'

'Yes, yes. Not bad, not bad. But vague, vague as ever.'

She was still in her bed, her white hair arranged in curls against the pink pillow. She was absent-mindedly tying and untying the ribbon of her nightdress. Madame Alvarez, pale, and as wan under her mourning hat as the moon behind the passing clouds, was leaning cross-armed against the bedside.

'And he added, "I don't wish to rush anything. Above all, I am Gigi's best pal. I shall give her all the time she wants to get used to me." There were tears in his eyes. And he also said, "After all, she won't have to deal with a savage." A gentleman, in fact. A perfect gentleman.'

'Yes, yes. Rather a vague gentleman. And the child, have you spoken frankly to her?'

'As was my duty, Alicia. This is no time for us to be treating her like a child from whom the cakes have to be hidden. Yes, I spoke to her frankly. I referred to Gaston as a miracle, as a god, as –'

'Tut, tut, tut,' criticized Alicia. 'I should have stressed the difficulties rather: the cards to be played, the fury of all those ladies, the conquest represented by so conspicuous a man.'

Madame Alvarez wrung her hands.

'The difficulties! The cards to be played! Do you imagine she's like you? Don't you know her at all? She's very far from calculating; she's –'

'Thank you.'

'I mean she has no ambition. I was even struck by the fact that she did not react either one way or the other. No cries of joy, no tears of emotion! All I got from her was. "Oh, yes! Oh, it's very considerate of him." Then, only at the very end, did she lay down as her conditions –'

'Conditions, indeed!' murmured Alicia.

'– that she would answer Monsieur Lachaille's proposals herself, and discuss the matter alone with him. In other words, it was her business, and hers only.'

'Let us be prepared for the worst! You've brought a half-wit into the world. She will ask for the moon and, if I know him, she won't get it. He is coming at four o'clock?'

'Yes.'

'Hasn't he sent anything? No flowers? No little present?'

'Nothing. Do you think that's a bad sign?'

'No. It's what one would expect. See that the child is nicely dressed. How is she looking?'

'Not too well today. Poor little lamb –'

'Come, come!' said Alicia heartlessly. 'You'll have time for tears another day – when she's succeeded in wrecking the whole affair.'

'You've eaten scarcely anything, Gigi.'

'I wasn't too hungry, Grandmamma. May I have a little more coffee?'

'Of course.'

'And a drop of Combier?'

'Why, yes. There's nothing in the world better than Combier for settling the stomach.'

Through the open window rose the noise and heat from the street below. Gigi let the tip of her tongue lick round the bottom of her liqueur glass.

'If Aunt Alicia could see you, Gigi!' said Madame Alvarez lightheartedly.

Gigi's only reply was a disillusioned little smile. Her old plaid dress was too tight across the breast, and under the table she stretched out her long legs well beyond the limits of her skirt.

'What can Mamma be rehearsing today that's kept her from coming back to eat with us, Grandmamma? Do you think there really is a rehearsal going on at her Opéra-Comique?'

'She said so, didn't she?'

'Personally, I don't think she wanted to eat here.'

'What makes you think that?'

Without taking her eyes off the sunny window, Gigi simply shrugged her shoulders.

'Oh, nothing, Grandmamma.'

When she had drained the last drop of her Combier, she rose and began to clear the table.

'Leave all that, Gigi. I'll do it.'

'Why, Grandmamma? I do it as a rule.'

She looked Madame Alvarez straight in the face, with an expression the old lady could not meet.

'We began our meal late, it's almost three o'clock and you're not dressed yet. Do pull yourself together, Gigi.'

'It's never before taken me a whole hour to change my clothes.'

'Won't you need my help? Are you satisfied your hair's all right?'

'It will do, Grandmamma. When the door-bell rings, don't bother, I'll go and open it.'

On the stroke of four, Gaston Lachaille rang three times. A childish, wistful face looked out from the bed-room door, listening. After three more impatient rings, Gilberte advanced as far as the middle of the hall. She still had on her old plaid dress and cotton stockings. She rubbed her cheeks with both fists, then ran to open the door.

'Good afternoon, Uncle Gaston.'

'Didn't you want to let me in, you bad girl?'

They bumped shoulders in passing through the door, said, 'Oh, sorry!' a little too self-consciously, then laughed awkwardly.

'Please sit down, Tonton. D'you know, I didn't have time to change. Not like you! That navy blue serge couldn't look better!'

'You don't know what your talking about! It's tweed.'

'Of course. How silly of me!'

She sat down facing him, pulled her skirt over her knees, and they stared at each other. Gilberte's tomboy assurance deserted her; a strange woebegone look made her blue eyes seem twice their natural size.

'What's the matter with you, Gigi?' asked Lachaille softly. 'Tell me something! Do you know why I'm here?'

She assented with an exaggerated nod.

'Do you want to, or don't you?' he asked, lowering his voice.

She pushed a curl behind her ear, and swallowed bravely. 'I don't want to.'

Lachaille twirled the tips of his moustache between two fingers, and for a moment looked away from a pair of darkened blue eyes, a pink cheek with a single freckle, curved lashes, a mouth unaware of its power, a heavy mass of ash-gold hair, and a neck as straight as a column, strong, hardly feminine, all of a piece, innocent of jewellery.

'I don't want what you want,' Gilberte began again. 'You said to Grandmamma...'

He put out his hand to stop her. His mouth was slightly twisted to one side, as if he had the toothache.

'I know what I said to your grandmother. It's not worth repeating. Just tell me what it is you don't want. You can then tell me what you do want. I shall give it to you.'

'You mean that?' cried Gilberte.

He nodded, letting his shoulders droop, as if tired out. She watched with surprise, these signs of exhaustion and torment.

'Tonton, you told Grandmamma you wanted to make me my fortune.'

'A very fine one,' said Lachaille firmly.

'It will be fine if I like it,' said Gilberte, no less firmly. 'They've drummed it into my ears that I am backward for my age, but all the same I know the meaning of words. "Make me my fortune": that means I should go away from here with you, and that I should sleep in your bed.'

'Gigi, I beg of you!'

She stopped because of the strong note of appeal in his voice.

'But, Tonton, why should I mind speaking of it to you? You didn't mind speaking of it to Grandmamma. Neither did Grandmamma mind speaking of it to me. Grandmamma wanted me to see nothing but the bright side. But I know more than she told me. I know very well that if you make me my fortune, then I must have my photograph in the papers, go to the Battle of Flowers and to the races at Deauville. When we quarrel, *Gil Blas* and *Paris en amour* will tell the whole story. When you throw me over once and for all, as you did Gentiane des Cevennes when you'd had enough of her —'

'What! You've heard about that? They've bothered your head with all those old stories?'

She gave a solemn little nod.

'Grandmamma and Aunt Alicia. They've taught me that you're world-famous. I know too that Maryse Chuquet stole your letters, and you brought an action against her. I know that Countess Pariewsky was angry with you because you didn't want to marry a *divorcée*, and she tried to shoot you. I know what all the world knows.'

Lachaille put his hand on Gilberte's knee.

'Those are not the things we have to talk about together, Gigi. All that's in the past. All that's over and done with.'

'Of course, Tonton, until it begins again. It's not your fault if you're world-famous. But I haven't got a world-famous sort of nature. So it won't do for me.'

In pulling at the hem of her skirt, she caused Lachaille's hand to slip off her knee.

'Aunt Alicia and Grandmamma are on your side. But as it concerns me a little, after all, I think you must allow me to say a word on the subject. And my word is, that it won't do for me.'

She got up and walked about the room. Gaston Lachailles' silence seemed to embarrass her. She punctuated her wanderings with 'After all, it's true, I suppose! No, it really won't do!'

'I should like to know,' said Gaston at last, 'whether you're not just trying to hide from me the fact that you dislike me. If you dislike me, you had better say so at once.'

'Oh no, Tonton, I don't dislike you at all! I'm always delighted to see you! I'll prove it by making a suggestion in my turn. You could go on coming here as usual, even more often. No one would see any harm in it, since you're a friend of the family. You could go on bringing me liquorice, champagne on my birthdays, and on Sunday we should have an extra special game of piquet. Wouldn't that be a pleasant little life? A life without all this business of sleeping in your bed and everybody knowing about it, losing strings of pearls, being photographed all the time and having to be so careful.'

She was absent-mindedly twisting a strand of her hair round her nose, and pulled it so tight that she snuffled and the tip of her nose turned purple.

'A very pretty little life, as you say,' interrupted Gaston Lachaille. 'You're forgetting one thing only, Gigi, and that is, I'm in love with you.'

'Oh!' she cried. 'You never told me that.'

'Well,' he answered uneasily. 'I'm telling you now.'

She remained standing before him, silent and breathing fast. There was no concealing her embarrassment; the rise and fall of her bosom under the tight bodice, the high colour on her cheeks, and the quivering of her close-pressed lips – albeit ready to open again and taste of life.

'That's quite another thing!' she cried at last. 'But then you are a terrible man! You're in love with me, and you want to drag me into a life where I'll have nothing but worries, where everyone gossips about everyone else, where the papers print nasty stories. You're in love with me, and you don't care a fig if you let me in for all sorts of horrible adventures, ending in separations, quarrels, Sandomirs, revolvers, and lau . . . and laudanum.'

She burst into violent sobs, which made as much noise as a fit of coughing. Gaston put his arms round her to bend her towards him like a branch, but she escaped and took refuge between the wall and the piano.

'But listen, Gigi! Listen to me!'

'Never! I never want to see you again! I should never have believed it of you. You're not in love with me, you're a wicked man! Go away from here!'

She shut him out from sight by rubbing her eyes with closed fists. Gaston had moved over to her and was trying to discover some place on her well-guarded face where he could kiss her. But his lips found only the point of a small chin wet with tears. At the sound of sobbing, Madame

Alvarez had hurried in. Pale and circumspect, she had stopped in hesitation at the door to the kitchen.

'Good gracious, Gaston!' she said. 'What on earth's the matter with her?'

'The matter!' said Lachaille. 'The matter is that she doesn't want to.'

'She doesn't want to!' repeated Madame Alvarez. 'What do you mean, she doesn't want to?'

'No, she doesn't want to. I speak plainly enough, don't I?'

'No. I don't want to,' whimpered Gigi.

Madame Alvarez looked at her granddaughter in a sort of terror.

'Gigi! It's enough to drive one raving mad! But I told you, Gigi. Gaston, as God is my witness, I told her –'

'You have told her too much!' cried Lachaille.

He turned his face towards the child, looking just a poor, sad, lovesick creature, but all he saw of her was a slim back shaken by sobs and a dishevelled head of hair.

'Oh!' he exclaimed hoarsely. 'I've had enough of this!' And he went out, banging the door.

The next day, at three o'clock, Aunt Alicia, summoned by *pneumatique*, stepped out from her hired brougham. She climbed the stairs up to the Alvarez' floor – pretending to the shortness of breath proper to someone with a weak heart – and noiselessly pushed open the door, which her sister had left on the latch.

'Where's the child?'

'In her room. Do you want to see her?'

'There's plenty of time. How is she?'

'Very calm.'

Alicia shook two angry little fists.

'Very calm! She has pulled the roof down about our heads, and she is very calm! These young people of today!'

Once again she raised her spotted veil and withered her sister with a single glance.

'And you, standing there, what do you propose doing?'

With a face like a crumpled rose, she sternly confronted

the large pallid face of her sister, whose retort was mild in the extreme.

'What do I propose doing? How do you mean? I can't after all, tie the child up!' Her burdened shoulders rose on a long sigh. 'I surely have not deserved such children as these!'

'While you stand there wringing your hands, Lachaille has rushed away from here and in such a state that he may do something idiotic!'

'And even without his straw hat,' said Madame Alvarez. 'He got into his motor bare-headed! The whole street might have seen him!'

'If I were to be told that by this time he's already become engaged, or is busy making it up with Liane, it would not surprise me in the least!'

'It is a moment fraught with destiny,' said Madame Alvarez lugubriously.

'And afterwards, how did you speak to that little chit?'

Madame Alvarez pursed her lips.

'Gigi may be a bit scatter-brained in certain things and backward for her age, but she's not what you say. A young girl who has held the attention of Monsieur Lachaille is not a little chit.'

A furious shrug of the shoulders set Alicia's black lace quivering.

'All right, all right! With all due respect, then, how did you handle your precious princess?'

'I talked sense to her. I spoke to her of the family. I tried to make her understand that we sink or swim together. I enumerated all the things she could do for herself and for us.'

'And what about nonsense? Did you talk nonsense to her? Didn't you talk to her of love, travel, moonlight, Italy? You must know how to harp on every string. Didn't you tell her that on the other side of the world the sea is phosphorescent, that there are humming-birds in all the flowers, and that you make love under gardenias in full bloom beside a moonlit fountain?'

Madame Alvarez looked at her spirited elder sister with sadness in her eyes.

'I couldn't tell her all that, Alicia, because I know nothing about it. I've never been farther afield than Cobourg and Monte Carlo.'

'Aren't you capable of inventing it?'

'No, Alicia.'

Both fell silent. Alicia, with a gesture, made up her mind.

'Call the chit in to me. We shall see.'

When Gilberte came in, Aunt Alicia had resumed all the airs and graces of a frivolous old lady and was smelling the tea-rose pinned near her chin.

'Good afternoon, my little Gigi.'

'Good afternoon, Aunt Alicia.'

'What is this Inez has been telling me? You have an admirer? And what an admirer! For your first attempt, it's a master-stroke!'

Gilberte acquiesced with a guarded, resigned little smile. She offered to Alicia's darting curiosity a fresh young face, to which the violet-blue shadow in her eyelids and the high colour of her mouth gave an almost artificial effect. For coolness' sake, she had dragged back the hair off her temples with the help of two combs, and this had drawn up the corners of her eyes.

'And it seems you have been playing the naughty girl, and tried your claws on Monsieur Lachaille! Bravo, my brave little girl!'

Gilberte raised incredulous eyes to her aunt.

'Yes, indeed! Bravo! It will only make him all the happier when you are nice to him again.'

'But I am nice to him, Aunt. Only, I don't want to, that's all.'

'Yes, yes, we know. You've sent him packing to his sugar refinery; that's perfect. But don't send him to the Devil; he's quite capable of going. The fact is, you don't love him.'

Gilberte gave a little childish shrug.

'Yes, Aunt, I'm very fond of him.'

'Just what I said, you don't love him. Mind you, there's

no harm in that, it leaves you free to act as you please. Ah, if you'd been head over heels in love with him, then I should have been a little anxious. Lachaille is a fine figure of a man. Well built – you've only to look at the photographs of him taken at Deauville in bathing costume. He's famous for that. Yes, I should feel sorry for you, my poor Gigi. To start by having a passionate love-affair – to go away all by your two selves to the other side of the world, forgetting everything in the arms of the man who adores you, listening to the song of love in an eternal spring – surely things of that sort must touch your heart! What does all that say to you?'

'It says to me that when eternal spring is over Monsieur Lachaille will go off with another lady. Or else that the lady – me if you like – will leave Monsieur Lachaille, and Monsieur Lachaille will hurry off to blab the whole story. And then the lady, still me if you like, will have nothing else to do but get into another gentleman's bed. I don't want that. I'm not changeable by nature, indeed I'm not.'

She crossed her arms over her breasts and shivered slightly.

'Grandmamma, may I have a *cachet Faivre*? I want to go to bed. I feel cold.'

'You great goose!' burst out Aunt Alicia, 'a tuppenny-ha'penny milliner's shop is all you deserve! Be off! Go and marry a bank clerk!'

'If you wish it, Aunt. But I want to go to bed.'

Madame Alvarez put her hand on Gigi's forehead.

'Don't you feel well?'

'I'm all right, Grandmamma. Only I'm sad.'

She leaned her head on Madame Alvarez' shoulder, and, for the first time in her life, closed her eyes pathetically like a grown woman. The two sisters exchanged glances.

'You must know, my Gigi,' said Madame Alvarez, 'that we won't torment you to that extent. If you say you really don't want to –'

'A failure is a failure,' said Alicia caustically. 'We can't go on discussing it for ever.'

'You'll never be able to say you didn't have good advice, and the very best at that,' said Madame Alvarez.

'I know, Grandmamma, but I'm sad, all the same.'

'Why?'

A tear trickled over Gilberte's downy cheek without wetting it, but she did not answer. A brisk peel of the door bell made her jump where she stood.

'Oh, it must be him,' she said. 'It is him! Grandmamma, I don't want to see him! Hide me, Grandmamma!'

At the low, passionate tone of her voice, Aunt Alicia raised an attentive head, and pricked an expert ear. Then she ran to open the door and came back a moment later. Gaston Lachaille, haggard, his eyes bloodshot, followed close behind her.

'Good afternoon, Mamita. Good afternoon, Gigi!' he said airily. 'Please don't move, I've come to retrieve my straw hat.'

None of the three women replied, and his assurance left him.

'Well, you might at least say a word to me, even if it's only How-d'you-do?'

Gilberte took a step towards him.

'No,' she said. 'You've not come to retrieve your straw hat. You have another one in your hand. And you would never bother about a hat. You've come to make me more miserable than ever.'

'Really!' burst out Madame Alvarez. 'This is more than I can stomach. How can you, Gigi! Here is a man who, out of the goodness of his generous heart –'

'If you please, Grandmamma, just a moment, and I shall have finished.'

Instinctively she straightened her dress, adjusted the buckle of her sash, and marched up to Gaston.

'I've been thinking, Gaston. In fact, I've been thinking a great deal –'

He interrupted her, to stop her saying what he was afraid to hear.

'I swear to you, my darling –'

'No, don't swear to me. I've been thinking I would rather be miserable with you than without you. So . . .'

She tried twice to go on.

'So . . . There you are. How d'you do, Gaston, how d'you do?'

She offered him her cheek, in her usual way. He held her, a little longer than usual, until he felt her relax, and become calm and gentle in his arms. Madame Alvarez seemed about to hurry forward, but Alicia's impatient little hand restrained her.

'Leave well alone. Don't meddle any more. Can't you see she is far beyond us?'

She pointed to Gigi, who was resting a trusting head and the rich abundance of her hair on Lachaille's shoulder.

The happy man turned to Madame Alvarez.

'Mamita,' he said, 'will you do me the honour, the favour, give me the infinite joy of bestowing on me the hand . . .'

The Cat

TRANSLATED BY
Antonia White

ONE

TOWARDS ten o'clock, the family poker-players began to show signs of weariness. Camille was fighting against sleepiness as one does at nineteen. By starts she would become fresh and clear-eyed again; then she would yawn behind her clasped hands and reappear pale, her chin white and her cheeks a little black under their ochre-tinted powder, with two tiny tears in the corners of her eyes.

'Camille, you ought to be in bed!'

'At ten o'clock, Mummy, at ten o'clock! Who on earth goes to bed at ten o'clock?'

Her eyes appealed to her fiancé, who lay back, overcome, in the depths of an armchair.

'Leave them alone,' said another maternal voice. 'They've still seven days to wait for each other. They're a bit dazed at the moment. It's very natural.'

'Exactly. One hour more or less ... Camille, you ought to go home to bed. So ought we.'

'Seven days!' cried Camille. 'But it's Monday today! And I hadn't given it a thought! Alain! Wake up! Alain!'

She threw her cigarette into the garden and lit a fresh one. Then she sorted out the scattered cards, shuffled them and laid them out as fortune-tellers do.

'To know whether we'll get the car, that marvellous baby roadster, before the ceremony! Look, Alain! I'm not cheating! It's coming out with a journey and an important piece of news!'

'What's that?'

'The roadster, of course!'

Without raising the nape of his neck from the chair, Alain turned his head towards the open french window, through which came the sweet smell of fresh spinach and new-mown hay. The grass had been shorn during the day, and the honeysuckle, which draped a tall dead tree, added the nectar of its first flowers to the scent of the cut grass.

A crystalline tinkle announced the entrance of the ten o'clock tray of soft drinks and iced water, carried by old Émile's tremulous hands, and Camille got up to fill the glasses.

She served her fiancé last, offering him the misted tumbler with a smile of secret understanding. She watched him drink and felt a sudden pang of desire at the sight of his mouth pressing against the rim of the glass. But he felt so weary that he refused to share that pang and merely touched the white fingers with the red nails as they removed his empty tumbler.

'Are you coming to lunch tomorrow?' she asked him under her breath.

'Ask the cards.'

Camille drew back quickly, and began to act the clown a little over her fortune-telling.

'Never, never joke about twenty-four-hours! Doesn't matter so much about crossed knives, or pennies with holes in them, or the talkies, or God the Father . . .'

'Camille!'

'Sorry, Mummy. But one mustn't joke about Twenty-four-hours! He's a good little chap, the knave of spades. A nice black express messenger, always in a hurry.'

'In a hurry to do what?'

'Why, to talk, of course! Just think, he brings the news of the next twenty-four hours, even of the next two days. If you put two more cards on his right and left, he foretells the coming week.'

She was talking fast, scratching at two little smudges of lipstick at the corners of her mouth with a pointed nail. Alain listened to her, not bored, but not indulgent either. He had known her for several years and classified her as a typical modern girl. He knew the way she drove a car, a little too fast and a little too well; her eye alert and her scarlet mouth always ready to swear violently at a taxi-driver. He knew that she lied unblushingly, as children and adolescents do; that she was capable of deceiving her parents so as to get out after dinner and meet him at a night-club. There they danced together, but they drank only orange-juice because Alain disliked alcohol.

Before their official engagement, she had yielded her discreetly-wiped lips to him both by daylight and in the dark. She had also yielded her impersonal breasts, always imprisoned in a lace brassière, and her very lovely legs in the flawless stockings she bought in secret; stockings 'like Mistinguett's, you know. Mind my stockings, Alain!' Her stockings and her legs were the best things about her.

'She's pretty,' Alain thought dispassionately, 'because not one of her features is ugly, because she's an out-and-out brunette. Those lustrous eyes perfectly match that sleek, glossy, frequently-washed hair that's the colour of a new piano.' He was also perfectly aware that she could be as violent and capricious as a mountain stream.

She was still talking about the roadster.

'No, Daddy, *no!* Absolutely no question of my letting Alain take the wheel while we're driving through Switzerland! He's too absent-minded. And besides, he doesn't really like driving. I know him!'

'She knows me,' Alain echoed in his own mind. 'Perhaps she really thinks she does. Over and over again, I've said to her too: "I know you my girl." Saha knows her too. Where is that Saha?'

His eyes searched round for the cat. Then, starting limb by limb, first one shoulder, then the other, he unglued himself from the armchair and went lazily down the five steps into the garden.

The garden was very large and surrounded by other gardens. It breathed out into the night the heavy smell of well-manured earth given over to producing flowers and constantly forced into fertility. Since Alain's birth, the house had hardly changed at all. 'An only son's house,' Camille said jeeringly. She did not hide her contempt for the high-pitched roof with the top-storey windows set in the slates and for certain modest mouldings which framed the french windows on the ground floor.

The garden, like Camille, also seemed to despise the house. Huge trees, which showered down the black, calcined twigs which fall from elms in their old age, protected it from neighbours and passers-by. A little farther on, in a property for sale and in the playground of a school, stood isolated pairs of similar old elms, relics of a princely avenue which had formed part of a park which the new Neuilly was fast destroying.

'Where are you, Alain?'

Camille was calling him from the top of the steps but, on an impulse, he refused to answer. Deliberately, he made for the safer refuge of the shadows, feeling his way along the edge of the shaven lawn with his foot. High in the sky a hazy moon held court, looking larger than usual through the mist of the first warm days. A single tree – a poplar with newly opened glossy leaves – caught the moonlight and trickled with as many sparkles as a waterfall. A silver shadow leapt out of a clump of bushes and glided like a fish against Alain's ankles.

'Ah! There you are, Saha! I was looking for you. Why didn't you appear at table tonight?'

'Me – rrou – wa,' answered the cat, 'me-rrou-wa.'

'What, me-rrou-wa? And why me-rrou-wa? Do you really mean it?'

'Me-rrou-wa,' insisted the cat, 'me-rrou-wa.'

He stroked her, tenderly groping his way down the long spine that was softer than a hare's fur. Then he felt under his hand the small, cold nostrils dilated by her violent purring. 'She's my cat. My very own cat.'

'Me–rrou–wa,' said the cat very softly. 'R . . . rrou–wa.'

Camille called once more from the house and Saha vanished under a clipped euonymus hedge, black-green like the night.

'Alain! We're going!'

He ran to the steps, while Camille watched him with a welcoming smile.

'I can see your hair running,' she called out. 'It's crazy to be as fair as all that!'

He ran quicker still, strode up the five steps in one bound, and found Camille alone in the drawing-room.

'Where are the others?' he asked under his breath.

'Cloakroom,' she whispered back. 'Cloakroom and visit to "work in progress". General gloom. "It's not getting on! It'll never be finished!" What the hell do we care! If one was smart, one could hold on to Patrick's studio for keeps. Patrick could find himself another. I'll fix it, if you like.'

'But Patrick would only leave the "Wedge" as a special favour to please *you*.'

'Of course. One will take advantage of that.'

Her face sparkled with that peculiarly feminine unscrupulousness which Alain could not bring himself to accept as a matter of course. But he remonstrated only on her habit of saying 'one' for 'we', and she took this as a reproach.

'I'll soon get into the way of saying "we".'

So that he should want to kiss her, she turned out the ceiling light as if by accident. The one lamp left alight on a table threw a tall, sharply defined shadow behind the girl.

With her arms raised and her hands clasped on the nape of her neck, Camille gave him an inviting look. But he had eyes only for the shadow. 'How beautiful she is on the wall! Just fine-drawn enough, just as I should like her to be.'

He sat down to compare the one with the other. Flattered, Camille arched herself, thrusting out her breasts and her hips like a nautch-girl, but the shadow was better at that game than she was. Unclasping her hands, the girl walked across the room, preceded by the ideal shadow. Arrived at the open french window, the shadow leapt on one side and fled out into the garden along the pink gravel of a path, embracing the moon-spangled poplar between its two long arms as it went. 'What a pity!' sighed Alain. Then he feebly reproached himself for his inclination to love in Camille herself some perfected or motionless image of Camille. This shadow, for example, or a portrait or the vivid memory she left him of certain moments, certain dresses.

'What's the matter with you tonight? Come and help me put on my cape, at least.'

He was shocked at what that 'at least' secretly implied and also because Camille, as she passed before him through the door leading to the cloakroom and pantry, had almost imperceptibly shrugged her shoulders. 'She doesn't need to shrug her shoulders. Nature and habit do that for her anyway. When she's not careful, her neck makes her look dumpy. Ever, ever so slightly dumpy.'

In the cloakroom they found Alain's mother and Camille's parents stamping as if with cold and leaving footmarks the colour of dirty snow on the matting. The cat, seated on the window-sill outside, watched them inhospitably but with no animosity. Alain imitated her patience and endured the ritual of pessimistic lamentations.

'It's the same old thing.'

'It's hardly any farther on than it was a week ago.'

'My dear, if you want to know what *I* think, it won't be a fortnight, it'll be a month. What am I talking about, a month? More likely two months before their nest . . .'

At the word 'nest', Camille flung herself into the peaceful fray so shrilly that Alain and Saha closed their eyes.

'But since we've already decided what to do! And since we're actually frightfully *pleased* at having Patrick's place! And since it suits Patrick down to the ground because he hasn't a bean – hasn't any money – sorry Mummy. We'll just take our suitcases and – Alley Oop! – straight up to heaven on the ninth floor! Won't we, Alain?'

He opened his eyes again, smiled into the void, and put her light cape round her shoulders. In the mirror opposite them he met Camille's black, reproachful look but it did not soften his heart. 'I didn't kiss her on the lips when we were alone. All right, very well then, I didn't kiss her on the lips. She hasn't had her full ration of kisses-on-the-lips today. She had the quarter-to-twelve one in the Bois, she had the two o'clock one after coffee, she had the half-past-six one in the garden, but she's missed tonight's. Well, if she's not satisfied, she's only got to put it down on the account ... What's the matter with me? I'm so sleepy, I'm going mad. This life's idiotic; we're seeing far too much of each other and yet we never see each other properly. On Monday I'll definitely go down to the shop and ...'

In imagination, the chemical acidity of the bales of new silk assailed his nostrils. But the inscrutable smile of M. Veuillet appeared to him as in a dream and, as in a dream, he heard words which, at twenty-four, he had still not learnt to hear without dread. 'No, no, my young friend. Will a new adding-machine that costs seventeen thousand francs pay back its initial outlay within the year? It all depends on that. Allow your poor father's oldest partner ...' Catching sight again in the looking-glass of the vindictive image and handsome dark eyes which were watching him, he folded Camille in both his arms.

'Well, Alain?'

'Oh, my dear, let him alone! These poor infants ...'

Camille blushed and disengaged herself. Then she held up her cheek to Alain in such a boyish brotherly grace that he nearly put his head on her shoulder. 'Oh, to lie down and go to sleep! Oh, good Lord! Just to lie down and sleep!'

From the garden came the voice of the cat.

'Me–rrou–wa ... Rrr–rrouwa.'

'Hark at the cat! She must be hunting,' said Camille calmly. 'Saha! Saha!'

The cat was silent.

'Hunting?' protested Alain. 'Whatever makes you think that? To begin with, we're in May. And then she's saying: "Me–rrou–wa!"'

'So what?'

'She wouldn't be saying "Me–rrou–wa" if she were hunting! What she's saying there – and it's really rather strange – means a warning. It's almost the cry calling her little ones together.'

'Good Lord!' cried Camille, flinging up her arms. 'If Alain's going to start interpreting the cat, we shall be here all night!'

She ran down the steps and, at the touch of old Émile's shaking hand, two old-fashioned gas-globes, like huge mauve planets, illuminated the garden.

Alain walked ahead with Camille. At the entrance gate, he kissed her under her ear, breathed in, under a perfume too old for her, a good smell of bread and dark hair, and squeezed the girl's bare elbows under her cape. When she seated herself at the steering-wheel, with her parents in the back, he felt suddenly wide awake and gay.

'Saha! Saha!'

The cat sprang out of the shadow, almost under his feet. When he began to run, she ran too, leaping ahead of him with long bounds. He guessed she was there without seeing her; she burst before him into the hall and came back to wait for him at the top of the steps. With her frill standing out and her ears low, she watched him running towards her, urging him on with her yellow eyes. Those deep-set eyes were proud and suspicious, completely masters of themselves.

'Saha! Saha!'

Pronounced in a certain way, under his breath, with the 'h' strongly aspirated, her name sent her crazy. She lashed her tail, bounded into the middle of the poker-table and, with her two cat's hands spread wide open, she scattered the playing-cards.

'That cat, that cat!' said his mother's voice. 'She hasn't the faintest notion of hospitality! Look how delighted she is that our friends have gone!'

Alain let out a spurt of childish laughter, the laugh he kept for home and the close intimacy which did not extend beyond the screen of elms or the black, wrought-iron gate. Then he gave a frantic yawn.

'Good heavens, how tired you look! Is it possible to

look as tired as that when one's happy? There's still some orangeade. No? We can go up then. Don't bother, Émile will turn out the lights.'

'Mother's talking to me as if I were getting over an illness or as if I were starting up paratyphoid again.'

'Saha! Saha! What a demon! Alain, you couldn't persuade that cat? . . .'

By a vertical path known to herself, marked on the worn brocade, the cat had almost reached the ceiling. One moment she imitated a grey lizard, flattening against the wall with her paws spread out; then she pretended to be giddy and tried an affected little cry of appeal. Alain obediently came and stood below and Saha slid down, glued to the wall like a raindrop sliding down a pane. She came to rest on Alain's shoulder and the two of them went up together to their bedroom.

A long hanging cluster of laburnum, black outside the open window, became a long pale yellow cluster when Alain turned on the ceiling light and the bedside lamp. He poured the cat off on to the bed by inclining his shoulder, then wandered aimlessly to and from between his room and the bathroom like a man who is too tired to go to bed.

He leaned out over the garden, looked with a hostile eye for the white mass of the 'alterations'. Then he opened and shut several drawers and boxes in which reposed his real secrets: a gold dollar, a signet ring, an agate charm attached to his father's watch chain, some red and black seeds from an exotic canna plant, a First Communicant's mother-of-pearl rosary and a thin broken bracelet, the souvenir of a tempestuous young mistress who had passed swiftly and noisily out of his life. The rest of his worldly goods consisted merely of some paper-covered books he had had rebound and some letters and autographs.

Dreamily he turned over these little scraps of wreckage, bright and worthless as the coloured stones one finds in the nests of pilfering birds. 'Should I throw all this away . . . or leave it here? It means nothing to me. Or does it mean something?' Being an only child, he was attached to everything which he had never shared with anyone else and for whose possession he had never had to fight.

He saw his face in the glass and became suddenly irritated with himself. 'Why can't you go to bed? You look a wreck. Positively disgraceful!' he said to the handsome fair young man. 'People only think me handsome because I'm fair. If I were dark, I'd be hideous.' For the hundredth time, he criticized his long cheeks and his slightly equine nose. But, for the hundredth time, he smiled so as to display his teeth to himself and admiringly touched the natural wave in his fair, over-thick hair. Once again he was pleased with the colour of his eyes, greenish-grey between dark lashes. Two dints hollowed his cheeks on either side of the smile, his eyes receded, circled with mauve shadows. He had shaved that morning but already a pale, stubbly bristle coarsened his upper lip. 'What a mug! I pity myself. No, I repel myself. Is *that* a face for a wedding night?' In the depths of the mirror, Saha gravely watched him from the distance.

'I'm coming, I'm coming.'

He flung himself on the cool expanse of the sheets, humouring the cat. Rapidly, he went through certain ritual litanies dedicated to the particular graces and virtues of a small, perfect, pure-bred Russian Blue.

'My little bear with the big cheeks. Exquisite, exquisite, exquisite cat. My blue pigeon. Pearl-coloured demon.'

As soon as he turned out the light, the cat began to trample delicately on her friend's chest. Each time she pressed down her feet, one single claw pierced the silk of the pyjamas, catching the skin just enough for Alain to feel an uneasy pleasure.

'Seven more days, Saha,' he sighed.

In seven days and seven nights he would begin a new life in new surroundings with an amorous and untamed young woman. He stroked the cat's fur, warm and cool at the same time and smelling of clipped box, thuya and lush grass. She was purring full-throatedly and, in the darkness, she gave him a cat's kiss, laying her damp nose for a second under Alain's nose between his nostrils and his lip. A swift, immaterial kiss which she rarely accorded him.

'Ah! Saha. Our nights...'

The headlights of a car in the nearest avenue pierced the leaves with two revolving white beams. Over the wall of the room passed the enlarged shadow of the laburnum and of a tulip-tree which stood alone in the middle of a lawn. Above his own face Alain saw Saha's face illuminated for a moment. Before it was eclipsed again, he had seen that her eyes were hard.

'Don't frighten me!' he implored.

For, when Alain was sleepy, he became once more weak and fanciful, caught in the mesh of a sweet and interminable adolescence.

He shut his eyes while Saha kept vigil, watching all the invisible signs which hover over sleeping human beings when the light is put out.

He always dreamed a great deal and descended into his dreams by definite stages. When he woke up, he did not talk about his adventures of the night. He was jealous of a realm which had been enlarged by a delicate and ill-governed childhood; by long sojourns in bed during his swift growth into a tall frail slender boy.

He loved his dreams and cultivated them. Not for anything in the world would he have revealed the successive stages which awaited him. At the first stopping-place, while he could still hear the motor-horns in the avenue, he met an eddy of faces, familiar yet distorted, which he passed through as he might have passed through a friendly crowd, geeting one here and there. Eddying, bulbous, the faces approached Alain, growing larger and larger. Light against a dark background, they became lighter still as if they received their illumination from the sleeper himself. Each was furnished with one great eye and they circled

round in an effortless gyration. But a submerged electric
current shot them far away as soon as they touched an
invisible barrier. In the humid gaze of a circular monster,
in the eye of a plump moon or that of a wild archangel with
rays of light for hair, Alain could recognize the same expression, the same intention which none of them had put
into words and which Alain of the dream noted with a
sense of security: 'They'll tell it me tomorrow.'

Sometimes they disappeared by exploding into scattered, faintly luminous fragments. At other times, they
only continued as a hand, an arm, a forehead, an eyeball
full of thoughts or as a starry dust of chins and noses. But
always there remained that prominent, convex eye which,
just at the moment of making itself clear, turned round
and exposed only its other, black surface.

The sleeping Alain pursued, under Saha's watchful
care, his nightly shipwreck. He passed beyond the world
of convex faces and eyes and descended through a zone
of darkness where he was conscious of nothing but a
powerful, positive blackness, indescribably varied and, as
it were, composed of submerged colours. On the confines
of this, he launched into the real, complete, fully-formed
dream.

He came up violently against a barrier which gave a
great clang like the prolonged, splintering clash of a
cymbal. And then he found himself in the dream city,
among the passers-by, the inhabitants standing in their
doorways, the gold-crowned guardians of the square and
the stage crowd posted along the path of an Alain who
was completely naked and armed with a walking-stick.
This Alain was extremely lucid and sagacious: 'If I walk
rather fast, after tying my tie in a special way, and particularly if I whistle, there's every chance that no one will
notice I am naked.' So he tied his tie in a heart-shaped knot
and whistled. 'That's not whistling, what I'm doing. It's
purring. Whistling's like this . . .' But he still continued to
purr. 'I'm not at the end of my tether yet. All I've got to
do . . . it's perfectly simple . . . is to cross this sun-drenched

open space and go round the bandstand where the military band is playing. Child's play. I run, making perilous jumps to distract attention, and I come out in the zone of shadow ...'

But he was paralysed by the warm, dangerous look of a dark man in the stage crowd; a young man with a Greek profile perforated by a great eye like a carp's. 'The zone of shadow ... the zone of *the* shadow...' Two long shadowy arms, graceful and rustling with poplar leaves appeared at the word 'shadow' and carried Alain away. During the most ambiguous hour of the short night, he rested in that provisional tomb where the living exile sighs, weeps, fights, and succumbs, and from which he rises, unremembering, with the day.

TWO

THE high sun was edging the window when Alain awoke. The newly-opened cluster of laburnum hung, translucid, above the head of Saha; a blue, diurnal Saha, innocently engaged in washing herself.

'Saha!'

'Me–rrang!' answered the cat aggressively.

'Is it my fault if you're hungry? You only had to go downstairs and ask for your milk if you're in a hurry.'

She softened at her friend's voice and repeated the same word less emphatically, showing her red mouth planted with white teeth. That look of loyal and exclusive love alarmed Alain: 'Oh heavens, this cat! What to do with this cat? I'd forgotten I was getting married. And that we've got to live in Patrick's place.'

He turned towards the photograph in the chromium frame where Camille gleamed as if covered in oil; a great splash of reflected light on her hair, her painted mouth vitrified in inky black, her eyes enormous between two palisades of eyelashes.

'Fine piece of studio portraiture,' muttered Alain.

He had quite forgotten that he himself had chosen this photograph for his room; a photograph which bore no resemblance to Camille or to anyone at all. 'That eye ... I've seen that eye.'

He took a pencil and lightly retouched the eye, toning down the excess of white. All he succeeded in doing was to spoil the print.

'Mouek, mouek, mouek. Ma-a-a-a ... Ma-a-a-a,' said Saha, addressing a little moth imprisoned between the window-pane and the net curtain.

Her leonine chin was trembling; she coveted it so much that she stammered. Alain caught the moth with two fingers and offered it to the cat.

'Hors-d'œuvre, Saha!'

In the garden, a rake was lazily combing the gravel.

Alain could see in his mind the hand that guided the rake; the hand of an ageing woman; a mechanical, obstinate hand in a huge white glove like a policeman's.

'Good morning, Mother!' he called.

A distant voice answered him, a voice whose words he did not try to catch; the affectionate, insignificant murmur was all that he needed. He ran downstairs, the cat at his heels. In broad daylight, she knew how to change herself into a kind of blustering dog. She would hurtle noisily down the stairs and rush into the garden with tomboyish jumps that had no magic about them. She seated herself on the little breakfast table, among the medallions of sunlight, beside Alain's plate. The rake, which had stopped, slowly resumed its task.

Alain poured out Saha's milk, stirred a pinch of salt and a pinch of sugar into it, then gravely helped himself. When he breakfasted alone, he did not have to blush for certain gestures elaborated by the unconscious wishes of the maniac age between six and seven. He was free to blind all the 'eyes' in his bread with butter and to frown when the coffee in his cup rose above the water-line marked by a certain gilt arabesque. A second thin slice had to follow the first thick slice, whereas the second cup demanded an extra lump of sugar. In fact a very small Alain, hidden in the depths of a tall, fair, handsome young man, was impatiently waiting for breakfast to be over so that he could lick both sides of the honey spoon; an old ivory spoon, blackened and flexible with age.

'Camille, at this moment, is eating her breakfast standing up. She's biting at one and the same time into a slice of lean ham squeezed between two rusks and into an American apple. And she keeps putting down a cup of tea without sugar in it on various bits of furniture and forgetting it.'

He raised his eyes and contemplated his domain; the domain of a privileged child which he cherished and whose every inch he knew. Over his head the old, severely pollarded elms stirred only the tips of their young leaves.

A cushiony mass of pink silene, fringed with forget-me-nots, dominated one lawn. Dangling like a scarf from the dead tree's scraggy elbow, a trail of polygonum intertwined with the four-petalled purple clematis fluttered in every breath of wind. One of the standard sprinklers spread a white peacock tail shot with a shifting rainbow as it revolved over the turf.

'Such a beautiful garden . . . such a beautiful garden,' said Alain under his breath. He stared disgustedly at the silent heaps of rubbish, timber, and bags of plaster which defaced the west side of the house. 'Ah! It's Sunday, so they're not working. It's been Sunday all the week for me.' Though young and capricious, and pampered, he now lived according to the commercial rhythm of a six-day week and felt Sunday in his bones.

A white pigeon moved furtively behind the weigela and the pink clusters of the deutzias. 'It's not a pigeon; it's mother's hand in her gardening glove.' The big white glove moved just above ground, raising a drooping stalk, weeding out the blades of grass that sprang up overnight. Two greenfinches came hopping along the gravel path to pick up the breakfast crumbs, and Saha followed them with her eye without getting excited. But a tomtit, hanging upside down in an elm above the table, chirped at the cat out of bravado. Sitting there with her paws folded, her head thrown back, and the frill of fur under her chin displayed like a pretty woman's jabot, Saha tried hard to restrain herself; but her cheeks swelled with fury and her little nostrils moistened.

'As beautiful as a fiend! More beautiful than a fiend!' Alain told her.

He wanted to stroke the broad skull in which lodged ferocious thoughts, and the cat bit him sharply to relieve her anger. He looked at the two little beads of blood on his palm with the irascibility of a man whose woman has bitten him at the height of her pleasure.

'Bad girl! Bad girl! Look what you've done to me!'

She lowered her head, sniffed the blood, and timidly

questioned her friend's face. She knew how to amuse him and charm him back to good humour. She scooped up a rusk from the table and held it between her paws like a squirrel.

The May breeze passed over them, bending a yellow rose-bush which smelt of flowering reeds. Between the cat, the rose-bush, the pairs of tomtits, and the last cockchafers, Alain had one of those moments when he slipped out of time and felt the anguished illusion of being once more back in his childhood. The elms suddenly became enormous, the path grew wider and longer and vanished under the arches of a pergola that no longer existed. Like the hag-ridden dreamer who falls off a tower, Alain returned violently to the consciousness of being nearly twenty-four.

'I ought to have slept another hour. It's only half-past nine. It's Sunday. Yesterday was Sunday for me too. Too many Sundays. But tomorrow . . .'

He smiled at Saha as though she were an accomplice. 'Tomorrow, Saha, there's the final trying-on of the white dress. Without me. It's a surprise. Camille's dark enough to look her best in white. During that time, I'll go and look at the car. It's a bit cheese-paring, a bit mingy, as Camille would say, a roadster. That's what you get for being "such a young married couple".'

With a vertical bound, rising in the air like a fish leaping to the surface of the water, the cat caught a black-veined cabbage-white. She ate it, coughed, spat out one wing, and licked herself affectionately. The sun played on her fur, mauve and bluish like the breast of a woodpigeon.

'Saha!'

She turned her head and smiled at him.

'My little puma! Beloved cat! Creature of the tree-tops! How will you live if we're separated? Would you like us to enter an Order? Would you like? . . . oh, I don't know what . . .'

She listened to him, watching him with a tender, absent expression. But when the friendly voice began to tremble, she looked away.

'To begin with, you'll come with us. You don't hate cars.
If we take the saloon instead of the roadster, behind the
seats there's a ledge . . .'

He broke off and became gloomy at the recent memory
of a girl's vigorous voice, ideally pitched for shouting in
the open air, trumpeting the numerous merits of the
roadster. 'And then, when you put down the windscreen,
Alain, its *marvellous*. When she's all out, you can feel the
skin of your cheeks shrinking right back to your *ears*.'

'Shrinking right back to your ears. Can you imagine anything more frightful, Saha?'

He compressed his lips and made a long face like an
obstinate child planning to get its own way by guile.

'It's not settled yet. Suppose I prefer the saloon? I
suppose I've got *some* say in the matter?'

He glared at the yellow rose-bush as if it were the young
girl with the resonant voice. Promptly the path widened,
the elms grew taller, and the non-existent pergola reappeared. Cowering among the skirts of two or three
female relatives, a childish Alain surveyed another com-
pact family among whose opaque block gleamed a very
dark little girl whose big eyes and black ringlets rivalled
each other in a hostile, jetty brilliance. 'Say "How d'you
do. . . ." Why don't you want to say "How d'you do?" ' It
was a faint voice from other days, preserved through years
of childhood, adolescence, college, the boredom of military service, false seriousness, false business competence.
Camille did not want to say 'How d'you do?' She sucked
the inside of her cheek and stiffly sketched the brief curtsy
expected of little girls. 'Now she calls that a "twist-your-
ankle" curtsy. But when she's in a temper, she still bites
the inside of her cheek. It's a funny thing, but at those
moments she doesn't look ugly.'

He smiled and felt an honest glow of warmth for his
fiancée. After all, he was quite glad that she should be
healthy and slightly commonplace in her sensuality. Defy-
ing the innocent morning, he called up images designed
now to excite her vanity and impatience, now to engender

anxiety, even confusion. Emerging from these disturbing
fancies, he found the sun too white and the wind dry.
The cat had disappeared but, as soon as he stood up, she
was at his side and accompanied him, walking with a long,
deerlike step and avoiding the round pebbles in the
pinkish gravel. They went together as far as the 'alterations' and inspected with equal hostility the pile of
rubbish, a new french window, devoid of panes, inserted
in a wall, various bathroom appliances, and some porce-
lain tiles.

Equally offended, they calculated the damage done to
their past and their present. An old yew had been torn
up and was very slowly dying upside down, with its roots
in the air. 'I ought never, never to have allowed that,'
muttered Alain. 'It's a disgrace. You've only known it for
three years, Saha, that yew. But I . . .'

At the bottom of the hole left by the yew, Saha sensed
a mole whose image, or rather whose smell went to her
head. For a minute she forgot herself to the point of frenzy,
scratching like a fox-terrier and rolling over like a lizard.
She jumped on all four paws like a frog, clutched a ball of
earth between her thighs as a fieldmouse does with the egg
it has stolen; escaped from the hole by a series of miracles,
and found herself sitting on the grass, cold and prudish
and recovering her breath.

Alain stood gravely by, not moving. He knew how to
keep a straight face when Saha's demons possessed her
beyond her control. The admiration and understanding
of cats was innate in him. Those inborn rudiments made
it easy for him, later on, to read Saha's thoughts. He had
read her like some masterpiece from the day, when on his
return from a cat-show, Alain had put down a little five-
months old she-cat on the smooth lawn at Neuilly. He had
brought her because of her perfect face, her precocious
dignity, and her modesty that hoped for nothing behind
the bars of a cage.

'Why didn't you buy a Persian instead?' asked Camille.
'That was long before we were engaged,' thought Alain.

'It wasn't only a little she-cat I bought. It was the nobility of all cats, their infinite disinterestedness, their knowledge of how to live, their affinities with the highest type of humans.' He blushed and mentally excused himself. 'The highest, Saha, is the one that understands *you* best.'

He had not yet got to the point of thinking 'likeness' instead of 'understanding' because he belonged to that class of human beings which refuses to recognize or even to imagine its animal affinities. But at the age when he might have coveted a car, a journey abroad, a rare binding, a pair of skis, Alain nevertheless remained the young-man-who-has-bought-a-little-cat. His narrow world resounded with it. The staff of Amparat et Fils in the Rue des Petits Champs were astonished and M. Veuillet inquired after the 'little beastie'.

'Before I chose you, Saha, I don't believe I'd ever realized that one *could* choose. As for all the rest . . . My marriage pleases everyone, including Camille. There are moments when it pleases me too, but . . .'

He got up from the green bench and assumed the important smile of the heir of Amparat Silks who is condescendingly marrying the daughter of Malmert Mangles, 'a girl who's not *quite* our type', as Mme Amparat said. But Alain was well aware that, when Malmert Mangles spoke about Amparat Silks among themselves, they did not forget to mention, sticking up their chins: 'The Amparats aren't in silk any more. The mother and son have only kept their shares in the business and the son's not the real director, only a figurehead.'

Cured of her madness, her eyes gentle and golden, the cat seemed to be waiting for the return of mental trust, of that telepathic murmur for which her silver-fringed ears were straining.

'You're not just a pure and sparkling spirit of a cat either,' went on Alain. 'What about your first seducer, the white tom without a tail? Do you remember that, my ugly one, my trollop in the rain, my shameless one?'

'What a bad mother your cat is!' exclaimed Camille indignantly. 'She doesn't even give a thought to her kittens, now they've been taken away from her.'

'But that was just what a young girl would say,' Alain went on defiantly. 'Young girls are always admirable mothers before they're married.'

The full, deep note of a bell sounded on the tranquil air. Alain leapt up with a guilty start at the sound of wheels crushing the gravel.

'Camille! It's half-past eleven ... Good Heavens!'

He pulled his pyjama jacket together and retied the cord so hastily and nervously that he scolded himself. 'Come, come, what's the matter with me? I shall be seeing plenty more of them in a week. Saha, are you coming to meet them?'

But Saha had vanished and Camille was already stamping across the lawn with reckless heels. 'Ah! She really does look attractive.' His blood pulsed pleasurably in his throat and flushed his cheeks. He was entirely absorbed in the spectacle of Camille in white, with a little lock of well-tapered hair on either temple and a tiny red scarf which matched her lipstick. Made-up with skill and restraint, her youth was not obvious at the first glance. Then it revealed itself in the cheek that was white under the ochre powder; in the smooth, unwrinkled eyelids under the light dusting of beige powder round the great eyes that were almost black. The brand-new diamond on her left hand broke the light into a thousand coloured splinters.

'Oh!' she cried. 'You're not ready! On a lovely day like this!'

But she stopped at the sight of the rough, dishevelled fair hair, of the naked chest under the pyjamas and Alain's flushed confusion. Her young girl's face so clearly expressed a woman's warm indulgence that Alain no longer dared to give her the quarter-to-twelve kiss of the Bois.

'Kiss me,' she implored, very low, as if she were asking him for help.

Gauche, uneasy and ill-protected by his thin pyjamas, he made a gesture towards the pink flowering shrubs from whence came the sound of the shears and the rake. Camille did not dare throw herself on his neck. She lowered her eyes, plucked a leaf, and pulled her shining locks of hair forward on her cheeks. But, from the movement of her nostrils, Alain saw she was searching in the air, with a certain primitive wildness, for the fragrance of a fair-skinned, barely-covered body. In his heart he secretly condemned her for not being sufficiently afraid of it.

THREE

WHEN he woke up, he did not sit up in bed at one bound. Haunted in his sleep by the unfamiliar room, he half-opened his eyes and realized that cunning and constraint had not entirely left him during his sleep, for his left arm, flung out across a desert of linen sheet, lay ready to recognize, but ready, also, to repel ... But all the wide expanse of bed to his left was empty and cool once more. If there had been nothing in front of the bed but the barely rounded corner of the triangular room and the unaccustomed green gloom, split by a rod of bright yellow light which separated two curtains of solid shadow, Alain would have gone to sleep again lulled by the sound of someone humming a little Negro song.

He turned his head cautiously and opened his eyes a trifle wider. He saw someone moving about, now white, now pale blue according to whether she was in the narrow strip of sunlight or the shadow. It was a naked young woman with a comb in her hand and a cigarette between her lips, wandering about the room and humming. 'What impudence,' he thought. 'Completely naked! Where does she think she is?'

He recognized the lovely legs with which he had long been familiar, but the stomach, shortened by a navel placed rather low, surprised him. An impersonal youthfulness justified the muscular buttocks and the breasts were small above the visible ribs. 'Has she got thinner, then?' The solidity of her back, which was as wide as her chest, shocked Alain. 'She's got a common back.' At that moment, Camille leaned her elbow on one of the window-sills, arched her back, and hunched up her shoulders. 'She's got a back like a charwoman.' But suddenly she stood upright again, took a couple of dancing steps and made a charming gestures of embracing the empty air. 'No, I'm wrong. She's beautiful. But what a . . . what brazenness; Does she think I'm dead? Or does it seem perfectly natural to her to wander about stark naked? Oh, but that will change!'

As she turned towards the bed, he closed his eyes again. When he opened them, Camille had seated herself at the dressing-table they called the 'invisible dressing-table', a transparent sheet of beautiful thick glass laid on a black metal frame. She powdered her face, touched her cheeks and chin with the tips of her fingers, and suddenly smiled, turning her eyes from the glass with a gravity and a weariness which disarmed Alain. 'Is she happy then? Happy about what? *I* certainly don't deserve it. But why is she naked?'

'Camille,' he called out.

He thought she would rush towards the bathroom, hastily covering herself with some hastily snatched-up undergarment. Instead, she ran to the bed and bent over the young man who lay there, overwhelming him with her strong brunette's smell.

'Darling! Have you slept well?'

'Stark naked!' he scolded.

She opened her big eyes comically.

'What about you?'

Bare to his waist, he did not know what to reply. She paraded for him, so proudly and so completely devoid of modesty that he rather rudely flung her the crumpled pyjama-jacket which lay on the bed.

'Quick, put that on. Personally, I'm hungry.'

'Old mother Buque's at her post. Everything's in working order and functioning.'

She disappeared and Alain wanted to get up and dress and smooth his rumpled hair. But Camille returned, girded in a big bathrobe that was new and too long for her, and gaily carrying a loaded tray.

'What a mess, my dears! There's a kitchen bowl and a pyrex cup and the sugar's in the lid of a tin. I'll get it all straightened out in a day or two. My ham's dry. These anaemic peaches are left-overs from lunch. Mother Buque's a bit lost in her electric kitchen. I'll teach her how to manage the various switches. Then I've put some water in the ice compartments of the 'fridge. It's a good thing I'm here! Monsieur has his coffee very hot and his milk boiling and his butter hard. No, that's my tea, don't touch! What are you looking for?'

'Nothing.'

Because of the smell of coffee, he was looking for Saha.

'What's the time?'

'At last a tender word!' cried Camille. 'Very early, my husband. It was a quarter-past eight by the kitchen alarm-clock.'

As they ate, they laughed a good deal and spoke little. By the increasing smell of the green oilcloth curtains, Alain could guess the strength of the sun which warmed them. He could not take his mind off that sun outside, the unfamiliar horizon, the nine vertiginous storeys, and the bizarre architecture of the 'Wedge' which was their temporary home.

He listened to Camille as attentively as he could, touched at her pretending to have forgotten what had passed between them in the night. He was touched, too, by her pretending to be perfectly at home in their haphazard lodging and by her unselfconsciousness, as if she had been married at least a week. Now that she had something on, he tried to find a way of showing his gratitude. 'She doesn't resent either what I've done to her or what I haven't, poor child. After all, the most tiresome part is over. Is it always like this the first night? This bruised, unsatisfactory feeling? This half-success, half-disaster?'

He threw his arm cordially round her neck and kissed her.

'Oh! You're nice!'

She had said it so loud and with so much feeling that she blushed and he saw her eyes fill with tears. But she bravely fought down her emotion and jumped off the bed on the pretext of removing the tray. She ran towards the windows, tripped over her long bathrobe, let out a great oath, and hauled on a ship's rope. The oilcloth curtains slid back. Paris, with its suburbs, bluish and unbounded like the desert, dotted with still-fresh verdure and flashes of shining panes, entered at one bound into the triangular room which had only one cement wall, the other two being half glass.

'It's beautiful,' said Alain softly.

But he was half lying and his head sought the support of a young shoulder from which the bathrobe had slipped. 'It's not a place for human beings to live. All this horizon right on top of one, right in one's bed. And what about stormy days. Abandoned on the top of a lighthouse among the albatrosses.'

Camille was lying beside him on the bed now. Her arm was round his neck and she looked fearlessly, now at the giddy horizons of Paris, now at the fair, dishevelled head. This new pride of hers which seemed to draw strength ahead from the coming night and the days that would follow, was no doubt satisfied with her newly-acquired rights. She was licensed to share his bed, to prop up a young man's naked body against her thigh and shoulder, to become acquainted with its colour and curves and defects. She was free to contemplate boldly and at length the small dry nipples, the loins she envied, and the strange design of the capricious sex.

They bit into the same tasteless peach and laughed, showing each other their splendid, glistening teeth and the gums which were a little pale, like tired children's.

'That day yesterday!' sighed Camille. 'When you think that there are people who get married so often!'

Her vanity returned and she added: 'All the same, it went off very well. Not a single hitch. It did go off well, didn't it?'

'Yes,' said Alain feebly.

'Oh, *you* ... You're just like your mother. I mean, as long as your lawn isn't ruined and people don't throw cigarette-ends on your gravel, you think everything's fine. Isn't that a fact? All the same, our wedding would have been prettier at Neuilly. Only that would have disturbed the sacred cat! Tell me, you bad boy, what do you keep looking at all round you?'

'Nothing,' he said sincerely, 'because there's nothing to look at. I've seen the dressing-table. I've seen the chair – we've seen the bed . . .'

'Couldn't you live here? I'd love to. Just think . . . three rooms and three balconies! If only one could stay here!'

'Doesn't one say: "If only *we* could stay here"?'

'Then why do *you* say: "One says"? Yes, if only one could stay here, as *we* say.'

'But Patrick will be back from his cruise in three months.'

'Who cares? He'll come back. And we'll explain that we want to stay on. And we'll chuck him out.'

'Oh! You'd actually do that?'

She shook her black mop affirmatively, with a radiant, feminine assurance in dishonesty. Alain wanted to give her a severe look but, under his eyes, Camille changed and became as nervous as he felt himself. Hastily he kissed her on the mouth.

Silent and eager, she returned his kiss, feeling for the hollow of the bed with a movement of her loins. At the same time her free hand, which was holding a peach-stone, groped in the air for an empty cup or ashtray.

Leaning over her, he caressed her lightly, waiting for her to open her eyes again.

She was pressing her eyelashes down over two small, glittering tears which she was trying to stop from flowing. He respected this restraint and this pride. They had done their best, the two of them, aided by the morning warmth and their two odorous, facile bodies.

Alain remembered Camille's quickened breathing and her warm docility. She had shown an untimely eagerness which was very charming. She reminded him of no other woman; in possessing her for the second time, he had thought only of the careful handling she deserved. She lay against him, her legs and arms relaxed, her hands half-closed, catlike for the first time. 'Where is Saha?'

Mechanically he gave Camille the ghost of a caress 'for

Saha', drawing his nails slowly and delicately all the way
down her stomach. She cried out with shock and stiffened
her arms. One of them hit Alain who nearly hit her back.
She sat up, with her hair on end and her eyes hostile and
threatening.

'Are you vicious, by any chance?'

He had expected nothing like this and burst out laughing.

'There's nothing to laugh about!' cried Camille. 'I've
always been told that men who tickle women are vicious.
They may even be sadists!'

He got off the bed so as to be able to laugh more freely,
quite forgetting he was naked. Camille stopped talking so
suddenly that he turned round and surprised her lit-up,
dazed face staring at the body of the young man whom one
night of marriage had made hers.

'D'you mind if I steal the bathroom for ten minutes?'

He opened the glass door let into one end of the longest
wall which they called the hypotenuse.

'And then I'll go over to my mother's for a moment.'

'Yes ... Don't you want me to come with you?'

He looked shocked and she blushed for the first time
that day.

'I'll see if the alterations . . .'

'Oh! the alterations! Don't tell me you're interested in
those alterations! Admit' – she folded her arms like a
tragic actress – 'admit that you're going to see my rival!'

'Saha's not your rival,' said Alain simply.

'How can she be your rival,' he went on to himself. 'You
can only have rivals in what's impure.'

'I don't need *such* a serious protestation, darling. Hurry
up! You haven't forgotten that we're lunching together
on our own at Père Léopold's? On our own at last, just the
two of us! You'll come back soon? You haven't forgotten
we're going for a drive? Are you taking in what I'm saying?'

What he took in very clearly was that the words 'come
back' had acquired a new and preposterous significance

and he looked at Camille askance. She was flaunting her newly-married bride's tiredness, drawing his attention to the faint swelling of her lower lids under the corners of her great eyes. 'Will you always have such enormous eyes the moment you wake up, whatever time of day or night? Don't you know how to keep your eyes half-closed? It gives me a headache to see eyes as wide open as all that.'

He felt a dishonest pleasure, an evasive comfort in calling her to account in his mind. 'After all, it's less ungracious than being frank.' He hurried to reach the square bathroom, the hot water, and a solitude propitious to thought. But, as the glass door inserted in the hypotenuse reflected him from head to foot, Alain opened it with complacent slowness and was in no haste to shut it again.

When he was leaving the flat an hour later, he opened the wrong door on one of the balconies which ran along every side of the Wedge. Like the sharp down-stroke of a fan, the east wind which was turning Paris blue, blowing away the smoke and scouring the distant Sacré Cœur, caught him full in the face. On the cement parapet, five or six pots, put there by well-meaning hands, contained white roses and hydrangeas and lilies sullied by their pollen. 'Last night's dessert is never attractive.' Nevertheless, before he went down, he sheltered the ill-treated flowers from the wind.

FOUR

HE stole into the garden like a boy in his teens who has stayed out all night. The air was full of the heady scent of beds being watered, of the secret exhalation of the filth which nourishes fleshy, expensive flowers and of spray blown on the breeze. In the very act of drawing a deep breath to inhale it all, he suddenly discovered he needed comforting.

'Saha! Saha!'

She did not come for a moment or two, and at first he did not recognize that bewildered, incredulous face which seemed clouded by a bad dream.

'Saha darling!'

He took her on his chest, smoothing the soft flanks which seemed to him a trifle hollow, and removed cobwebs, pine needles, and elm twigs from the neglected fur. She pulled herself together quickly and resumed her familiar expression and her cat's dignity. Her face, her pure golden eyes looked again as he had known them. Under his thumb, Alain could feel the palpitations of a hard, irregular little heart and also the beginnings of a faint, uncertain purr. He put her down on an iron table and stroked her head. But at the moment of thrusting her head into Alain's hand, wildly and as if for life in the way she had, she sniffed that hand and stepped back a pace.

His eyes sought the white pigeon, the gloved hand behind the pink flowering shrubs, behind the flaming rhododendrons. He rejoiced that yesterday's 'ceremony' had respected the beautiful garden and only ravaged Camille's home.

'Imagine those people here! And those four bridesmaids in pink paper! And the flowers they'd have picked, and the deutzias sacrificed to adorn fat women's bosoms! And Saha!'

He called in the direction of the house: 'Has Saha had

anything to eat or drink? She looks awfully queer. I'm here, Mother.'

A heavy white shape appeared in the doorway of the hall and answered from the distance: 'No. Just fancy, she had no supper and wouldn't drink her milk this morning. I think she was waiting for you. Are you all right, dear?'

He stood at the foot of the steps, deferential in his mother's presence. He noticed that she did not offer him her cheek as usual and that she kept her hands clasped together at her waist. He understood and shared this motherly sense of decency with a mixture of embarrassment and gratitude. 'Saha hasn't kissed me either.'

'After all, the cat's often seen you go away. She made allowances for your going off sometimes.'

'But I didn't go so far,' he thought.

Near him, on the iron table, Saha drank her milk avidly like an animal that has walked far and slept little.

'Alain, wouldn't you like a cup of warm milk too? Some bread and butter?'

'I've had breakfast, Mother. *We've* had breakfast.'

'Not much of a breakfast, I imagine. In such a glory-hole!'

With the eye of an exile, Alain contemplated the cup with the gilt arabesque beside Saha's saucer; then his mother's heavy face, amiable under the mass of wavy, prematurely white hair.

'I haven't asked you whether my new daughter is satisfied.' She was frightened he would misunderstand her and added hurriedly: 'I mean, whether she's in good health.'

'Excellent, Mother. We're going out to Rambouillet for lunch in the forest. I've got to run the car in,' He corrected himself: '*We've* got to run the car in, I mean.'

They remained alone together in the garden, he and Saha, both torpid with silence and weariness and overcome with longing to sleep.

The cat fell asleep suddenly on her side, her chin up and her teeth bared like a dead animal. Feathery panicles from the Venetian sumach and clematis petals rained down on her without her so much as twitching in the depths of the dream in which, no doubt, she was enjoying the security of her friend's inalienable presence. Her defeated attitude, the pale, drawn corners of her periwinkle-grey lips gave evidence of a night of miserable watching.

Above the withered stump draped with climbing plants, a flight of bees over the ivy-flowers gave out a solemn cymbal note, the identical note of so many summers. 'To go to sleep out here, on the grass, between the yellow rose-bush and the cat. Camille won't come till dinner-time, that will be very pleasant. And the cat, good heavens, the cat ...' Over by the 'alterations' could be heard the rasp of a plane shaving a beam, the clang of an iron hammer on a metal girder, and Alain promptly embarked on a dream about a village peopled with mysterious blacksmiths. As eleven sounded from the belfry of the school near by, he got up and fled without daring to wake the cat.

FIVE

JUNE came with its longer days, its night skies devoid of mystery which the late glow of the sunset and the early glimmer of dawn over the east of Paris kept from being wholly dark. But June is cruel only to city-dwellers who have no car and are caged up in hot stone and forced to live elbow to elbow. A never-still breeze played round the Wedge, rippling the yellow awnings. It blew through the triangular room and the studio, broke against the prow of the building, and dried up the little hedges of privet that stood in boxes on the balconies. With the help of their daily drives, Alain and Camille lived pleasantly enough. The warm weather and their sensual life combined to make them drowsy and less exacting with each other.

'Why did I call her an untamed girl?' Alain asked himself in surprise. Camille swore less when she was driving the car and had lost certain crudities of speech. She had also lost her passion for night-clubs with female gipsy singers who had nostrils like horses.

She spent much time eating and sleeping, opened her now much gentler eyes very wide, gave up a dozen summer projects, and became interested in the 'alterations' which she visited daily. Often she lingered long in the garden at Neuilly, where Alain, when he came back from the dark offices of Amparat Fils in the Rue des Petits-Champs, would find her idle, ready to prolong the afternoon and drive along the hot roads.

Then his mood would darken. He would listen to her giving orders to the singing painters and the distant electricians. She would question him in a general, peremptory way as if, as soon as he was there, it was her duty to renounce her new gentleness.

'Business going all right? Crisis still expected? Have you managed to put over the spotted foulard on the big dress-houses?'

She did not even respect old Émile, whom she shook until he let fall certain formulas pregnant with oracular imbecility.

'What do you think of our shanty, Émile? Have you ever seen the house looking so nice?'

Between his whiskers, the old butler muttered answers as shallow and colourless as himself.

'You wouldn't know the place any more. Had anyone told me, in the old days, that this house would be divided up into little compartments . . . There's certainly a difference. It will be very nice being so near each other, very gay.'

Or else, drop by drop, he poured a stream of blessings over Alain, blessings in which there was an under-current of hostility.

'Monsieur Alain's young lady is beginning to look ever so well. What a fine voice she has. When she's speaking loud, the neighbours can hear every word. You can't deny she has a splendid voice but . . . The young lady speaks her mind all right. She told the gardener that the bed of pink silene and forget-me-not looked cuckoo. I still have to laugh when I think of it.'

And he raised his pale, oyster-coloured eyes, which had never laughed in their life, to the pure sky. Alain did not laugh either. He was worried about Saha. She was getting thinner and seemed to have given up a hope; undoubtedly the hope of seeing Alain every day again – and alone. She no longer ran away when Camille arrived. But she did not escort Alain to the gate and, when he sat by her, she looked at him with a profound and bitter wisdom. 'Her look when she was a little cat behind the bars. The same, same look.' He called her very softly: 'Saha . . . Saha . . .' strongly aspirating the 'h's. But she did not jump or flatten her ears and it was days since she had given her insistent: 'Me-rrang'! or the 'Mouek-mouek-mouek' of good humour and greed.

One day, when he and Camille had been summoned to Neuilly to be informed that the enormous, heavy, new sunk bath would cave in the tiled platform supporting it, he heard his wife sigh: 'It'll never be finished!'

'But,' he said, surprised, 'I thought you really much preferred the Wedge with its petrels and cormorants.'

'Yes. But all the same . . . And after all it's your house here, your real house. *Our* house.'

She leaned on his arm, rather limp and unusually hesitant. The bluish whites of her eyes, almost as blue as her light summer dress; the unnecessary but admirable make-up of her cheeks and mouth and eyelids did not move him in the least.

Nevertheless, it seemed to him that, for the first time, she was asking his advice without speaking. 'Camille here with me. So soon! Camille in pyjamas under the rose trellis.' One of the oldest climbing roses carried its load of flowers, which faded as soon as they opened, as high as his head and their oriental scent dominated the garden in the evening; he could smell it where they stood by the steps. 'Camille in a bathrobe under the screen of elms. Wouldn't it be better, all things considered, to keep her shut away in the little gazebo of the Wedge? Not here, not here . . . not yet.'

The June evening, drenched with light, was reluctant to give way to darkness. Some empty glasses on a wicker table were still attracting the big orange bumble-bees but, under all the trees except the pines, an area of impalpable damp was growing, bringing a promise of coolness. Neither the rose geraniums, so prodigal of their southern scent upon the air, nor the fiery poppies suffered from the fierce onslaught of summer. 'Not here, not here.' Alain repeated to the rhythm of his own footsteps. He was looking for Saha and did not want to call her out loud. He found her lying on the little low wall which buttressed a blue knoll covered with lobelias. She was asleep, or appeared to be asleep, curled up in a ball. 'Curled up in a ball? At this time and in this weather? Sleeping curled up like that is a winter position!'

'Saha darling!'

She did not quiver as he picked her up and held her in the air. She only opened two hollow eyes, very beautiful and almost indifferent.

'Heavens, how light you are! But you're ill, my little puma!'

He carried her off and ran back to his mother and Camille.

'But, Mother, Saha's ill! Her coat's shocking – she weighs next to nothing – and you never told me!'

'It's because she eats nothing,' said Mme Amparat. 'She refuses to eat.'

'She doesn't eat? And what else?'

He cradled the cat against his chest and Saha abandoned herself to him. Her breathing was shallow and her nostrils dry. Mme Amparat's eyes, under the thick white waves, glanced intelligently at Camille.

'Nothing else,' she said.

'She's bored with you,' said Camille. 'After all she's your cat, isn't she?'

He thought she was laughing at him and raised his head defiantly. But Camille's face had not changed and she was seriously examining Saha, who shut her eyes again as soon as touched by her.

'Feel her ears,' said Alain sharply. 'They're burning.'

In an instant, his mind was made up.

'Right. I'm taking her with me. Mother, get them to fetch me her basket, will you? And a sack of sand for the tray. We've got everything else she needs. You understand I simply couldn't bear ... This cat believes ...'

He broke off and turned belatedly to his wife.

'It won't worry you, Camille, if I take Saha while we're waiting to come back here?'

'What a question! But where do you propose to put her at night?' she added so naïvely that Alain blushed because of his mother's presence and answered acridly: 'That's for her to decide.'

They left in a little procession; Alain carrying Saha,

mute in her travelling-basket. Old Émile was bowed under the sack full of sand and Camille brought up the rear, bearing an old frayed kasha travelling rug which Alain called the Kashasaha.

SIX

'No, I never thought a cat would get acclimatized so quickly.'

'A cat's merely a cat. But Saha's Saha.'

Alain was proudly doing the honours of Saha. He himself had never kept her so close at hand, imprisoned in twenty-five square metres and visible at all hours. For her feline meditation, for her craving for solitude and shadow, she was reduced to withdrawing under the giant armchairs scattered about the studio or into the miniature hall or into one of the built-in wardrobes camouflaged with mirrors.

But Saha was determined to triumph over all obstacles. She accepted the uncertain times of meals and of getting up and going to bed. She chose the bathroom with its cork-topped stool to sleep in and she explored the Wedge with no affectation of wildness or disgust. In the kitchen, she condescended to listen to the lazy voice of Mme Buque summoning 'the pussy' to raw liver. When Alain and Camille went out, she installed herself on the giddy parapet and gazed into the abysses of air, following the flying backs of swallows and sparrows below her with a calm, untroubled eye. Her impassiveness on the edge of a sheer drop of nine storeys and the habit she had of washing herself at length on the parapet, terrified Camille.

'Stop her,' she yelled to Alain. 'She makes my heart turn over and gives me cramp in my calves.'

Alain gave an unperturbed smile and admired his cat who had recovered her taste for food and life.

It was not that she was blooming or particularly gay. She did not recover the iridescence of her fur that had gleamed like a pigeon's mauve plumage. But she was more alive; she waited for the dull 'poum' of the lift which brought up Alain and accepted extra attentions from Camille, such as a tiny saucer of milk at five o'clock or a small chicken bone offered high up, as if to a dog who was expected to jump for it.

'Not like that! Not like that!' scolded Alain.

And he would lay the bone on a bathmat or simply on the thick-piled beige carpet.

'Really . . . on Patrick's carpet!' Camille scolded in turn.

'But a cat can't eat a bone or any solid food on a polished surface. When a cat takes a bone off a plate and puts it down on the carpet before eating it, she's told she's dirty. But the cat needs to hold it down with her paw while she crunches and tears it and she can only do it on bare earth or on a carpet. People don't know that.'

Amazed, Camille broke in: 'And how do *you* know?'

He had never asked himself that and got out of it by a joke: 'Hush! It's because I'm extremely intelligent. Don't tell a soul. M. Veuillet hasn't a notion of it.'

He taught her all the ways and habits of the cat, like a foreign language over-rich in subtle shades of meaning. In spite of himself, he spoke with emphatic authority as he taught. Camille observed him narrowly and asked him any number of questions which he answered unreservedly.

'Why does the cat play with a piece of string when she's frightened of the big ship's rope?'

'Because the ship's rope is the snake. It's the thickness of a snake. She's afraid of snakes.'

'Has she ever seen a snake?'

Alain looked at his wife with the grey-green, black-lashed eyes she found so beautiful . . . 'So treacherous' she said.

'No . . . certainly not. Where could she have seen one?'

'Well, then?'

'Well, then she invents one. She creates one. You'd be frightened of snakes too, even if you'd never seen one.'

'Yes, but I've been told about them. I've seen them in pictures. I know they exist.'

'So does Saha.'

'But how?'

He gave her a haughty smile.

'How? But by her birth, like persons of quality.'

'So I'm not a person of quality?'

He softened, but only out of compassion.

'Good Heavens, no. Console yourself: I'm not either. Don't you believe what I tell you?'

Camille, sitting at her husband's feet, contemplated him with her wildest eyes, the eyes of the little girl of other days who did not want to say 'How d'you do?'

'I'd better believe it,' she said gravely.

They took to dining at home nearly every night, because of the heat, said Alain, 'and because of Saha' insinuated Camille. One evening after dinner, Saha was sitting on her friend's knee.

'What about me?' said Camille.

'I've two knees,' Alain retorted.

Nevertheless, the cat did not use her privilege for long. Some mysterious warning made her return to the polished ebony table where she seated herself on her own bluish reflection immersed in a dusky pool. There was nothing unusual about her behaviour except the fixed attention she gave to the invisible things straight in front of her in the air.

'What's she looking at?' asked Camille.

She was pretty every evening at that particular hour; wearing white pyjamas, her hair half loosened on her forehead and her cheeks very brown under the layers of powder she had been superimposing since the morning. Alain sometimes kept on his summer suit, without a waistcoat, but Camille laid impatient hands on him, taking off his jacket and tie, opening his collar and rolling up his shirt-sleeves, seeking and displaying the bare skin. He treated her as a hussy, letting her do as she wished. She laughed a little unhappily as she contained her feelings. And it was he who lowered his eyes with an anxiety that was not entirely voluptuous. 'What ravages of desire on that face! Her mouth is quite distorted with it. A young wife who's so *very* young. Who taught her to forestall me like that?'

The round table, flanked by a little trolley on rubber wheels, gathered the three of them together at the entrance to the studio, near the open bay window. Three tall old poplars, relics of a beautiful garden that had been destroyed, waved their tops at the height of the balcony and the great setting sun of Paris, dark red and smothered in mists, was going down behind their lean heads from which the sap was retreating.

Mme Buque's dinner – she cooked food well and served it badly – enlivened the hour. Refreshed, Alain forgot his day and the Amparat office and the tutelage of M. Veuillet. His two captives in the glass tower made a fuss of him. 'Were you waiting for me?' he murmured in Saha's ear.

'I heard you coming!' cried Camille. 'One can hear every sound from here!'

'Have you been bored?' he asked her one evening, fearing that she was going to complain. But she shook her black mop in denial.

'Not the least bit in the world. I went over to Mummy's. She's presented me with the treasure.'

'What treasure?'

'The little woman who'll be my maid over there. Provided old Émile doesn't give her a baby. She's quite attractive.'

She laughed as she rolled up her white crêpe sleeves over her bare arms before she cut open the red-fleshed melon round which Saha was tiptoeing. But Alain did not laugh: he was too taken up with the horror of imagining a new maid in his house.

'Yes? But do you remember,' he brought out, 'my mother's never changed her servants since I was a child.'

'That's obvious,' said Camille trenchantly. 'What a museum of old crocks!'

She was biting into a crescent of melon as she spoke and laughing, with her face to the setting sun. Alain admired, in a detached way, how vivid a certain cannibal radiance could be in those glittering eyes and on the glittering teeth in the narrow mouth. There was something Italian about her regular features. He made one more effort to be considerate.

'You never see your girl friends nowadays, it seems to me. Mightn't you perhaps...'

She took him up fiercely.

'And what girl friends, may I ask? Is this your way of telling me I'm a burden on you? So that I shall give you a little breathing space. That's it, isn't it?'

He raised his eyebrows and clicked his tongue 'tst... tst'. She yielded at once with a plebeian respect for the man's disdain.

'It's quite true. I never had any friends when I was a little girl. And now... can you see me with a girl who's not married. Either I'd have to treat her as a child or I'd have to answer all her dirty questions: "And what does one do *here* and how does he do *that* to you!" Girls,' she explained with some bitterness, 'girls don't stick together decently. There's no solidarity. It's not like all you men.'

'Forgive me! I'm not one of "all-you-men"!'

'Oh, I know that all right,' she said sadly. 'Sometimes I wonder if I wouldn't rather...'

She was very rarely sad and, when she was, it was because of some secret reticence or some doubt that she did not express.

'*You* haven't any friends either,' she went on. 'Except Patrick and he's away. And even Patrick, you don't really care a damn about him.'

She broke off at a gesture from Alain.

'Don't let's talk about these things,' she said intelligently. 'There'll only be a quarrel.'

The long-drawn-out cries of children rose from the ground level and blended with the airy whistling of the swallows. Saha's beautiful yellow eyes, in which the great nocturnal pupil was slowly invading the iris, stared into space, picking out moving, floating, invisible points.

'Tell me, whatever's the cat looking at? Are you sure there's nothing, over there where she's staring?'

'Nothing... for us.'

Alain evoked with regret the faint shiver, the seductive fear that his cat friend used to communicate to him in the days when she slept on his chest at night.

'She doesn't make you frightened, I hope?' he said condescendingly.

Camille burst out laughing, as if the insulting word were just what she had been waiting for.

'Frightened? There aren't many things that frighten *me*, you know!'

'That's the statement of a silly little fool,' said Alain angrily.

'Let's say you're feeling the storm coming, shall we?' said Camille, shrugging her shoulders.

She pointed to the wall, purpled with clouds which were coming up with the night.

'And you're like Saha,' she added. 'You don't like storms.'

'No one likes storms.'

'I don't hate them,' said Camille judicially. 'Anyway, I'm not the slightest bit afraid of them.'

'The whole world is afraid of storms,' said Alain, hostile.

'All right, I'm not the whole world, that's all.'

'You are for me,' he said with a sudden, artificial grace which did not deceive her.

'Oh!' she scolded under her breath. 'I shall hit you.'

He bent his fair head towards her over the table and showed his white teeth.

'All right, hit me!'

But she deprived herself of the pleasure of rumpling that golden hair and offering her bare arm to those shining teeth.

'You've got a crooked nose,' she flung at him fiercely.

'It's the storm,' he said, laughing.

This subtlety was not at all to Camille's taste, but the first low rumblings of the thunder distracted her attention. She threw down her napkin to run out on the balcony.

'Come along! There'll be some marvellous lightning.'

'No,' said Alain, without moving. 'Come along, yourself.'

'Where to?'

He jerked his chin in the direction of their room. Camille's face assumed the obstinate expression, the dull-witted greed he knew so well. Nevertheless, she hesitated.

'But couldn't we look at the lightning first?'

He made a sign of refusal.

'Why not, horrid?'

'Because *I'm* frightened of storms. Choose. The storm or . . . me.'

'What do you think!'

She ran to their room with an eagerness which flattered Alain's vanity. But, when he joined her there, he found she had deliberately lighted a luminous glass cube near the vast bed. He deliberately turned it out.

The rain came in through the open bay-windows as they lay calm again, warm and tingling, breathing in the ozone that filled the room with freshness. Lying in Alain's arms, Camille made him understand that, while the storm raged, she would have liked him once again to forget his terror of it with her. But he was nervously counting the great sheets of lightning and the tall dazzling trees silhouetted against the cloud and he moved away from Camille. She resigned herself, raised herself on her elbow and combed her husband's crackling hair with one hand. In the pulsations of the lightning-flashes their two blue plaster faces rose out of the night and were swallowed up in it again.

'We'll wait till the storm's over,' she consented.

'And *that*,' said Alain to himself, '*that's* what she finds to say after an encounter that really means something. She might at least have kept quiet. As Émile says, the young lady speaks her mind straight out.'

A flickering flash, long as a dream, was reflected in a blade of fire in the thick slab of glass on the invisible dressing-table. Camille clutched Alain against her bare leg.

'Is that to reassure me? We know you're not frightened of lightning.'

He raised his voice so as to be heard above the hollow rumbling and the rain cascading on the flat roof. He felt tired and on edge, tempted to be unjust yet frightened to say openly that nowadays he was never alone. In his mind he returned violently to his old room with its white wallpaper patterned with stiff conventional flowers, a room which no one had ever tried to make prettier or uglier. His longing for it was so fierce that the murmur of the inefficient old radiator came back with the memory of the pale flowers on the wallpaper. The wheezy mutter that came from the hollow space below its copper pipes seemed to be part of the murmurs of the whole house; of the whispering of the worn old servants, half-buried in their basement, who no longer cared to go out even into the garden. ... 'They used to say "She" when they talked about my mother but I've been "Monsieur Alain" since I first went into knickerbockers.'

A dry crackle of thunder roused him from the brief doze into which he had fallen. His young wife, leaning over him, propped on her elbow, had not stirred.

'I like you so much when you're asleep,' she said. 'The storm's going off.'

He took this as a demand and sat up.

'I'm following its example,' he said. 'How hot and sticky it is! I'm going to sleep on the waiting-room bench.'

The 'waiting-room bench' was their name for the narrow divan which was the solitary piece of furniture in a tiny room, a mere strip of glass-walled passage which Patrick used for sunbathing.

'Oh, no! Oh, no!' implored Camille. 'Do stay.'

But he had already slipped out of the bed. The great flashes in the clouds revealed Camille's hard, offended face.

'Pooh! Baby boy!'

At this, which he was not expecting, she pulled his nose. With an instinctive reflex of his arm, which he could not control and did not regret, he beat down the disrespectful hand. A sudden lull in the wind and rain left them alone in the silence, as if struck dumb. Camille massaged her hand.

'But ...' she said at last, 'But ... you're a brute.'

'Possibly,' said Alain. 'I don't like having my face

touched. Isn't the rest of me enough for you? Never touch my face.'

'But you *are* . . . you really *are* a brute,' Camille repeated slowly.

'Don't keep on saying it. Apart from that, I've nothing against you. Just mind you don't do it again.'

He lifted his bare leg back on to the bed.

'You see that big grey square on the carpet? It's nearly daybreak. Shall we go to sleep?'

'Yes . . . let's . . .' said the same, hesitant voice.

'Come on, then !'

He stretched out his left arm so that she could rest her head on it. She did so submissively and with a circumspect politeness. Pleased with himself, Alain gave her a friendly jostle and pulled her towards him by her shoulder. But he bent his knees a little to keep her at a safe distance and fell asleep almost at once. Camille lay awake, breathing carefully, and watched the grey patch on the carpet growing lighter. She listened to the sparrows celebrating the end of the storm in the three poplars whose rustling sounded like the faint continuation of the rain. When Alain, changing his position, withdrew his arm, he gave her an unconscious caress. Three times his hand slid lightly over her head as if accustomed to stroking fur that was even softer than her soft black hair.

SEVEN

IT was towards the end of June that incompatibility became established between them like a new season of the year. Like a season, it had its surprises and even its pleasures. To Alain, it was like a harsh, chilly spring inserted in the heart of summer. He was incessantly and increasingly aware of his repugnance at the idea of making a place for this young woman, this outsider, in his own home. He nursed this resentment and fed it with secret soliloquies and the sullen contemplation of their new dwelling. Camille, exhausted with the heat, called out from the high and now windless balcony: 'Oh, let's chuck everything. Let's take the old scooter and go somewhere where we can bathe. Shall we, Alain?'

'All right by me,' he answered with wily promptitude. 'Where shall we go?'

There was a peaceful interlude while Camille enumerated beaches and names of hotels. With his eye on Saha who lay flat and prostrated, Alain had the leisure to think and to conclude: 'I don't want to go away with her I . . . I daren't. I'm quite willing to go for a drive, as we used to, and come back in the evening or late at night. But that's all. I don't want evenings in hotels and nights in a casino, evenings of . . .' He shuddered: 'I need time. I realize that I take a long time to get used to things, that I'm a difficult character, that . . . But I don't want to go off with *her*.' He felt a pang of shame as he realized that he had mentally said '*her*' just like Émile and Adèle when they were discussing 'Madame' in undertones.

Camille bought road-maps and they played at travelling through a France spread in quarters over the polished ebony table which reflected their two blurred, inverted faces.

They added up the mileage, ran down their car, cursed each other affably and felt revived, even rehabilitated by a comradeship they had forgotten. But tropical showers, unaccompanied by gales, drowned the last days of June and the balconies of the Wedge. Sheltering behind the closed panes, Saha watched the level rivulets, which Camille mopped up by stamping on table-napkins, winding across the inlaid tiles. The horizon; the city; the shower itself; all took on the colour of clouds loaded with inexhaustible rain.

'Would you rather we took the train?' suggested Alain suavely.

He had foreseen that Camille would fly out at the detested word. Fly out she did indeed – and blasphemously.

'I'm afraid,' he went on, 'that you're getting bored. All those trips we'd promised ourselves.'

'All those summer hotels. All those restaurants full of flies. All those seas full of people bathing,' she railed plaintively. 'Look here, you and I are quite used to driving around. But what we're good at is just going for drives. We're quite lost when it comes to a real journey.'

He saw that she was slightly depressed and gave her a brotherly kiss. But she turned round and bit him on his mouth and under his ear. Once again, they fell into the diversion which shortens the hours and makes the body attain its pleasure easily. It was beginning to make Alain tired. When he dined at his mother's with Camille and had to stifle his yawns, Mme Amparat lowered her eyes and Camille invariably gave a little, swaggering laugh. For she was proudly conscious of the habit Alain had acquired of making love to her hurriedly and almost peevishly, flinging her away the moment it was over to return to the cool side of the uncovered bed.

Ingenuously, she would rejoin him there and he did not forgive her for that although, silently, he would yield again. After that he felt at liberty to probe at leisure into the sources of what he called their incompatibility. He was wise enough to put these outside their frequent love-making. Clear-headed, helped by the very fact of his sexual exhaustion, he returned to those retreats where the hostil-

ity of man to woman keeps its unageing freshness. Sometimes she revealed herself to him in some common-place
realm where she slept in broad sunshine, like an innocent
creature. Sometimes he was astonished, even scandalized,
that she should be so dark. Lying in bed behind her, he
surveyed the short hairs on her shaved neck, ranged like
the prickles of a sea-urchin and drawn on the skin like the
hatching on a map. The shortest of them were blue and
visible under the fine skin before each one emerged through
a small blackened pore.

'Have I never really had a dark woman?' he wondered.
'Two or three little black-haired things haven't left me any
impression of *such* darkness.' And he held his own arm up
to the light. It was yellowish-white; a typical fair man's arm
with green-gold down and jade-coloured veins. His own
hair seemed to him like a forest with violet shadows, whereas Camille's showed the strange whiteness of the skin between the exotic abundance of those ranks of black, slightly
crinkled stalks.

The sight of a fine, very black hair stuck to the side of a
basin made him feel sick. Then the little neurosis changed
and, abandoning the detail, he concentrated on her whole
body. Holding that young, appeased body in his arms in
the night which hid its contours he began to be annoyed
that a creative spirit, in moulding Camille, had shown a
strict reasonableness like that of his English nurse. 'Not
more prunes than rice, my boy,' she used to say. 'Not more
rice than chicken.' That spirit had modelled Camille ade-
quately but with no concessions to lavishness or fantasy.
He carried his annoyances and regrets into the ante-
chamber of his dreams during that incalculable moment
reserved for the black landscape peopled with bulbous
eyes, fish with Greek noses, moons and chins. There he de-
sired a big-hipped charmer of the 1900 type, liberally developed above a tiny waist, to compensate for the acid
smallness of Camille's breasts. At other times, half asleep,
he compromised and preferred a top-heavy bosom; two
quivering, monstrous hillocks of flesh with sensitive tips.

Such feverish desires, which were born of the sexual act
and survived it, never affronted the light of day nor even
complete wakefulness. They merely peopled a narrow
isthmus between nightmare and voluptuous dream.

When her flesh was warm, the 'foreigner' smelt of wood
licked by tongues of flame; birch, violets ... a whole
bouquet of sweet, dark tenacious scents which clung long
to the palms. These fragrances produced in Alain a kind
of perverse excitement but did not always arouse his
desire.

'You're like the smell of roses,' he said one day to Camille, 'you take away one's appetite.'

She looked at him dubiously and assumed the slightly
gauche, downcast expression with which she received
double-edged compliments.

'How awfully eighteen-thirty you are,' she murmured.

'You're much more so,' replied Alain. 'Oh, ever so much
more so. I know who you're like.'

'Marie Dubas, the actress. I've been told that before.'

'Hopelessly wrong, my girl! Minus the bandeaux, you're
like all those girls who weep on the tops of towers in the
works of Loïsa Puget. You can see them weeping on the
cover of his romantic songs, with *your* great, prominent
Greek eyes and those thick rims to the lower lid that makes
the tears jump down on to the cheeks ...'

One after another, Alain's senses took advantage of him
to condemn Camille. He had to admit, at least, that she
stood up admirably to certain remarks he fired at her point-
blank. They were provocative rather than grateful remarks
that burst out of him at the times when, lying on the floor,
he measured her with narrowed eyes and appraised her
new merits without indulgence or regard for her feelings.
He judged her particular aptitudes; he noted how that
sensual ardour of hers, that slightly monotonous passion,
had already developed an enlightened self-interest re-
markable in so young a married woman. Those were
moments of frankness and certainty and Camille did all

she could to prolong their half silent atmosphere of conflict; their tension like that of a tight-rope on which balance was precarious and dangerous.

Having no deep-seated malice in herself, Camille never suspected that Alain was only half taken in by deliberate challenges, pathetic appeals and even by a cool Polynesian cynicism, and that each time he possessed his wife, he meant it to be the last. He mastered her as he might have put a hand on her mouth to stop her from screaming or as he might have murdered her.

When she was dressed again and sitting upright beside him in their roadster, he could look at her closely without rediscovering what it was that had made her his worst enemy. As soon as he regained his breath, listening to his decreasing heartbeats, he ceased to be the dramatic young man who stripped himself naked before wrestling with his companion and overthrowing her. The brief routine of pleasure; the controlled expert movements, the real or simulated gratitude were relegated to the ranks of what is over, of what will probably never happen again. Then his greatest preoccupation would return, the one which he accepted as natural and honourable, the question which reassumed the first place it had so long deserved: 'How to stop Camille from living in MY house?'

Once this period of hostility towards the 'alterations' had passed, he had genuinely put his faith in the return to the home of his childhood, in the tranquillizing influence of a life on ground level; a life in contact with the earth and everything the earth brings forth. 'Here, I'm suffering from living up in the air. Oh, to see branches and birds from *underneath* again!' he sighed. But he concluded severely 'Pastoral life is no solution', and once more had recourse to his indispensable ally, the lie.

On a blazing afternoon which melted the asphalt he went to his domain. All about it, Neuilly was a desert of the empty roads and empty tramways of July; the gardens were abandoned except for a few yawning dogs. Before leaving Camille, he had installed Saha on the coolest balcony of the Wedge. He was vaguely worried every time he left his two females alone together.

The garden and the house were asleep and the little iron gate did not creak as he opened it. Overblown roses, red poppies, the first ruby-throated Canna lilies and dark snap-dragons burned in isolated clumps on the lawns. At the side of the house gaped the new doorway and two new windows in a freshly-painted little one-storey building. 'It's all finished,' Alain realized. He walked carefully, as he did in his dreams, and trod only on the grass.

Hearing the murmur of a voice rising from the base-ment, he stopped and absent-mindedly listened. It was only the old well-known voices of servility and ritual grumbling, the old voices which used to say 'She' and 'Monsieur Alain'. Once upon a time they had flattered the fragile, fair-haired little boy and his childish pride ... 'I was a king, once,' Alain said to himself, smiling sadly.

'Well, so *she'll* soon be coming to sleep here, I suppose?' one of the old voices asked audibly.

'That's Adèle,' thought Alain. Leaning against the wall, he listened without the least scruple.

'Of course she will,' bleated Émile. 'That flat's shock-ingly badly built.'

The housemaid, a greying Basque woman with a hairy face, broke in: 'You're right there. From their bathroom you can hear everything that goes on in the water-closet. Monsieur Alain won't like *that*.'

'*She* said, the last time *she* came that *she* didn't need curtains in her little drawing-room because there are no neighbours on the garden side.'

'No neighbours? What about us when we go to the wash-house? What's one going to see when *she*'s with Monsieur Alain?'

Alain could guess the smothered laughter and the ancient Émile continued: 'Oh, perhaps one won't see as much as all *that*. *She*'ll be put in her place, all right. Monsieur Alain's not the sort to let himself go on a sofa at any time of day or night.'

There was a silence during which Alain could hear nothing but the sound of a knife on the grindstone. But he stayed listening, with his back against the hot wall and his eyes vaguely searching between a flaming geranium and the acid green of the turf as if he half-expected to see Saha's moonstone-coloured fur.

'As for me,' said Adèle, 'I think it's oppressive, that scent *she* puts on.'

'And her frocks,' supplemented Juliette, the Basque woman. 'The way she dresses isn't really good style. *She* looks more like an actress. Behaves like one too, with that brazen way of hers. And now what's she going to land us with in the way of a lady's maid? Some creature out of an orphanage, I believe, or worse.'

A fanlight slammed and the voices were cut off. Alain felt weak and trembling. He breathed like a man who has just been spared by a gang of murderers. He was neither surprised nor indignant. There was not much difference between his own opinion of Camille and that of the harsh judges in the basement. But his heart was beating fast because he had meanly eavesdropped without being punished for it and because he had been listening to prejudiced witnesses and unsought accomplices. He wiped his face and took a deep breath as if inhaling this gust of misogyny, this pagan incense offered exclusively to the male principle, had anaesthetized him. His mother, who had just wakened from her siesta and was putting back the shutters of her room, saw him standing there, with his cheek still leant against the wall.

She called softly, like a wise mother.

'Ah! my boy . . . Is anything the matter?'

He took her hands over the window-sill, like a lover.

'Nothing at all. I was out for a walk and just thought I'd look in.'

'A very good idea.'

She did not believe him but they smiled at each other, perfectly aware that neither was telling the truth.

'Mother, could I ask you to do me a little favour?'

'A little favour in the way of money, isn't that it? I know you're none too well off this year, my poor children.'

'No, Mother. Please, would you mind not telling Camille that I came here today? As I didn't come here for any special reason, I mean with no special reason except just to look in and give you a kiss. I'd rather ... Actually, that's not all. I want you to give me some advice. Strictly between the two of us, you know.'

Mme Amparat lowered her eyes, ran her hand through her wavy white hair, and tried to avert the confidence.

'I'm not much of a talker, as you know. You've caught me all untidy. I look like an old gipsy. Won't you come inside into the cool?'

'No, Mother. Do you think there's any way ... it's an idea I can't get out of my head ... a polite way, of course ... something that wouldn't offend anyone ... but some way of stopping Camille from living here?'

He seized his mother's hands, expecting them to tremble or to draw away But they stayed, cold and soft, between his own.

'These are just a young husband's ideas,' she said, embarrassed.

'What do you mean?'

'With young married couples, things go too well or they go too badly. I don't know which works out best in the end. But they never go straightforwardly, just of their own accord.'

'But, Mother, that's not what I'm asking you. I'm asking you whether there isn't any way ...'

For the first time, he was unable to look his mother in the face. She gave him no help and he turned away irritably.

'You're talking like a child. You run about the streets in this frightful heat and you come to me after a quarrel and ask me impossible questions. *I* don't know. Questions whose only answer is divorce. Or moving house. Or heaven knows what.'

She got breathless whenever she talked and Alain only

reproached himself for making her flush and pant even at saying so little. 'That's enough for today,' he thought prudently.

'We haven't had a quarrel, Mother. It's only I who can't get used to the idea . . . who doesn't want to see . . .'

With a wide, embarrassed gesture, he indicated the garden that surrounded them: the green lake of the lawn; the bed of fallen petals under the rose arches; a swarm of bees over the flowering ivy; the ugly, revered house.

The hand he had kept in one of his clenched and hardened into a little fist and he suddenly kissed that sensitive hand: 'Enough, that's enough for today.'

'I'm off now, Mother. Monsieur Veuillet's telephoning you at eight tomorrow about this business of the shares going down. Do I look better now, Mother?'

He raised his eyes that looked greener in the shade of the tulip-tree and threw back his face which from habit, affection, and diplomacy he had forced into his old childish expression. A flutter of the lids to brighten the eye, the seductive smile, a little pout of the lips. His mother's hand unclenched again and reached over the sill to feel Alain's well-known weak spots; his shoulder-blades, his Adam's apple, the top of his arm. She did all this before replying.

'A little better. Yes, really, quite a lot better.'

'I've pleased her by asking her to keep something secret from Camille.' At the remembrance of his mother's last caress, he tightened his belt under his jacket. 'I've got thinner, I'm getting thinner. No more physical culture – no physical culture other than making love.'

He went off with a light step, in his summer clothes, and the cooling breeze dried his sweat and blew the acrid smell of it ahead of him. He left his native castle inviolate, his subterranean cohort intact, and the rest of the day would pass easily enough. Until midnight, no doubt, sitting in the car beside an inoffensive Camille, he would drink in the evening air, now sylvan as they drove between oak plantations edged with muddy ditches, now dry and smelling of wheatstraw. 'And I'll bring back some fresh couch-grass for Saha.'

Vehemently, he reproached himself for the lot of his cat who lived so soundlessly at the top of their glass tower. 'She's like her own chrysalis, and it's my fault.' At the hour of their conjugal games she banished herself so rigorously that Alain had never seen her in the triangular room. She ate just sufficient to keep alive; she had lost her varied language and given up all her demands, seeming to prefer her long waiting to everything else. 'Once again, she's waiting behind bars. She's waiting for me.'

Camille's shattering voice came through the closed door as he reached the landing.

'It's that filthy bloody swine of an animal! I wish it were dead! What? No, Madame Buque, I don't care what you say. To hell with it! To hell with it!'

He made out a few more violent expressions. Very softly he turned the key in the lock but, once over his own threshold, he could not consent to listen without being seen. 'A filthy bloody swine of an animal? But what animal? An animal in the house?'

In the studio Camille, wearing a little sleeveless pullover and a knitted béret miraculously balanced on her skull, was furiously pulling a pair of gauntlet gloves over her bare hands. She seemed stupefied at the sight of her husband.

'It's you! Where have you sprung from?'

'I haven't sprung from anywhere. I've simply arrived home. Who are you so furious with?'

She avoided the trap and neatly turned the attack on Alain.

'You're very cutting, the first time you get home punctually. *I'm* ready. I've been waiting for you.'

'You haven't been waiting for me since I'm punctual to the minute. Who were you so angry with? I heard "filthy bloody swine of an animal?" What animal?'

She squinted very slightly but sustained Alain's look.

'The dog!' she cried. 'That damned dog downstairs, the

dog that barks morning, noon, and night. It's started again! Can't you hear it barking? Listen!'

She raised her finger to make him keep quiet and Alain had time to notice that the gloved finger was shaking. He yielded to a naïve need to make sure.

'Just fancy, I thought you were talking about Saha.'

'Me?' cried Camille. 'Me speak about Saha in that tone? Why I wouldn't dare! The heavens would fall if I did! For goodness' sake, are you coming?'

'Go and get the car out, I'll join you down below. I've just got to get a handkerchief and a pullover.'

His first thought was to find the cat. On the coolest balcony, near the deck-chair in which Camille occasionally slept in the afternoon, he could see nothing but some fragments of broken glass. He stared at them blankly.

'The cat's with me, Monsieur,' came the fluting voice of Mme Buque. 'She's very fond of my wicker stool. She sharpens her claws on it.'

'In the kitchen,' thought Alain painfully. 'My little puma, my cat of the garden, my cat of the lilacs and the butterflies, in the kitchen! Ah! All that's going to change!'

He kissed Saha on the forehead and chanted some ritual praises, very low. He promised her couch-grass and sweet acacia flowers. But he found both the cat and Mme Buque artificial and constrained; Mme Buque in particular.

'We may be back to dinner and we may not, Madame Buque. Has the cat everything she needs?'

'Yes, Monsieur. Oh yes, indeed, Monsieur,' said Mme Buque hurriedly. 'I do everything I possibly can, really I do, Monsieur!'

The big, fat woman was red in the face and seemed on the verge of tears. She ran a friendly, clumsy hand over the cat's back. Saha arched her back and proffered a little 'm'hain', the mew of a poor timid cat which made her friend's heart swell with sadness.

The drive was more peaceful than he had hoped. Sitting at the wheel, her eyes alert, her feet and hands perfectly synchronized, Camille drove him as far as the slope of Montfort-l'Amaurey.

'Shall we have dinner out-of-doors, Alain? Shall we, Alain, darling?'

She smiled at him in profile, beautiful as she always was in the twilight; her cheek brown and transparent, her teeth and the corner of her eye the same glittering white. In the forest of Rambouillet, she put down the windscreen and the wind filled Alain's ears with a sound of leaves and running water.

'A little rabbit! . . .' cried Camille. 'A pheasant!'

'It's still a rabbit . . . One moment more and I . . .'

'He doesn't know his luck, that chap!'

'You've got a dimple in your cheek like you have in your photos as a child,' said Alain, beginning to come to life.

'Don't talk about it! I'm getting enormous!' she said, shaking her shoulders.

He watched for the return of the laugh and the dimple, and his eyes wandered down to the robust neck, free of any trace of the 'girdle of Venus', the round, inflexible neck of a handsome white Negress. 'Yes, she really has got fatter. And in the most seductive way. For her breasts, those too . . .' He withdrew into himself once more and came up, morosely, against the age-old male grievance. 'She's getting fat from making love. She's battening on *me*.' He slipped a jealous hand under his jacket, felt his ribs, and ceased to admire the childish dimple in her cheeks.

But he felt a certain gratified vanity when they sat down a little later at a famous inn and the neighbouring diners stopped talking and eating to stare at Camille. And he exchanged with his wife the smiles, the movements of the chin and all the rituals of coquetry suitable to a 'handsome couple'.

However, it was only for him that Camille lowered her voice and displayed a certain languor and certain charming attentions which were not in the least for show. In revenge, Alain snatched out of her hand the dish of raw tomatoes and the basket of strawberries, insisted that she ate chicken with a cream sauce, and poured her out a wine which she did not care for but which she drank fast.

'You know perfectly well I don't like wine,' she repeated each time she emptied her glass.

The sun had set but the sky was still almost white, dappled with small deep-pink clouds. But night and cool-ness seemed to be rising as one from the forest which loomed, massive, beyond the tables of the inn. Camille laid her hand on Alain's.

'What is it? What is it? What's the matter?' he said in terror.

Astonished, she withdrew her hand. The little wine she had drunk gleamed gaily in her eyes in which shone the tiny, quivering image of the pink balloons hung from the pergola.

'Nothing's the matter, silly. You're as nervous as a cat! Is it forbidden for me to put my hand on yours?'

'I thought,' he admitted weakly, 'I thought you wanted to tell me something ... something serious ... I thought,' he burst out with it, 'you were going to tell me you were pregnant.'

Camille's shrill little laugh attracted the attention of the men at the near-by tables.

'And you were as overcome as all that? With joy or ... fed-up-ness?'

'I don't exactly know. What about you? Would you be pleased or not pleased? We've hardly thought about it ... at least, *I* haven't. But what are you laughing at?'

'Your face! All of a sudden, a face as if you were just going to be hanged. It's too funny. You'll make my eye-black come unstuck.'

With her two forefingers, she lifted up either eyelid.

'It isn't funny, it's serious,' said Alain, glad to put her in the wrong. 'But why was I so terrified?' he thought.

'It's only serious,' said Camille, 'for people who've got nowhere to live or who've only got two rooms. But people like us ...'

Serene, lulled into optimism by the treacherous wine,

she smoked and talked as if she were by herself, her thigh against the table and her legs crossed.

'Pull down your skirt, Camille.'

She did not hear him and went on: 'We've got all the essentials a child needs. A garden – and what a garden! And a dream of a room with its own bathroom.'

'A room?'

'Your old room. We'd have it repainted. And it would be very nice of you not to insist on a frieze of little ducks and fir trees on a sky-blue background. That would ruin the taste of our offspring.'

He restrained himself from stopping her. She was talking at random, her cheeks flushed, as she stared into the distance, seeing all she was building up. He had never seen her so beautiful. He was fascinated by the base of her neck, like the smooth unwrinkled bole of a tree, and by the nostrils which were blowing out smoke. 'When I give her pleasure and she tightens her lips, she opens her nostrils like a little horse as she breathes.

He heard such crazy predictions fall from the reddened scornful lips that they ceased to alarm him: Camille was calmly proceeding with her woman's life among the wreckage of Alain's past. 'Good Lord,' he thought. 'How she's got it all organized. I'm certainly learning something!' A tennis-court was to replace the great, useless lawn. The kitchen and the pantries . . .

'Haven't you ever realized how inconvenient they are? And think of all that wasted space. It's like the garage. I'm only saying all this, darling, so as you should know I think a lot about our real setting up house. Above all, we must be tactful with your mother. She's so awfully sweet . . . we mustn't do anything she wouldn't approve of. Must we?'

He put in haphazard 'Yesses' and 'Noes' as he picked up some wild strawberries scattered on the cloth. After hearing her say 'your old room', he had been immunized by a provisional calm, a foretaste of indifference.

'Only one thing may make things awkward for us,'

Camille went on. 'Patrick's last postcard dated from the Balearic Isles. Do pay attention! It'll take less time for Patrick to get back from the Balearics than for our decorator to get everything finished. I hope he comes to a violent end, that son of Penelope by a male tortoise! But I shall put on my siren voice: "Patrick, my pet . . ." You know my siren voice makes a tremendous impression on Patrick.'

'From the Balearic Isles . . .' broke in Alain thoughtfully. 'From the Balearic Isles.'

'Otherwise practically from next door. Where are you off to? Do you want us to go? It was so nice here.'

Her brief intoxication was over. She stood up shivering and yawning with sleepiness.

'I'll drive,' said Alain. 'Put on the old coat that's under the cushion. And go to sleep.'

A flak of flying insects, bright silver moths and stag-beetles hard as pebbles, whirled in front of the headlights and the car drove back the wing-laden air like a wave. Camille did indeed go to sleep, sitting perfectly upright. She was trained not to encumber the driver's arm and shoulder, even in her sleep. She merely gave a little forward jerk of her head at every jolt in the road.

'From the Balearic Isles,' Alain kept repeating to himself. The dark air, the white fires which caught and repulsed and decimated the flying creatures took him back to the populous threshold of his dreams; the sky with its stardust of exploded faces, the great hostile eyes which put off till tomorrow a reckoning, a password or a significant figure. He was so deep in that world that he forgot to take the short cut between Pontchartrain and the Versailles toll-gate and Camille scolded him in her sleep. 'Bravo!' applauded Alain. 'Good reflex action! Good little faithful, vigilant senses. Ah, how much I like you, how well we get on, when you're asleep and I'm awake.'

Their sleeves and their unprotected hair were wet with dew when they set foot in their newly-built street, empty in the moonlight. Alain looked up; nine storeys up, in the middle of the almost round moon, the little horned shadow of a cat was leaning forward, waiting.

'Look! Look how she's waiting!'

'You've got good eyes,' said Camille, yawning.

'If she were to fall! Whatever you do, don't call her!'

'You needn't worry,' said Camille. 'If I did call her, she wouldn't come.'

'For good reason,' said Alain unpleasantly.

As soon as he had said it, he was angry with himself. 'Too soon, too soon! And what a bad moment to choose!' Camille dropped the hand that was just about to push the bell.

'For good reason? For what good reason? Come on, out with it. I've been lacking in respect to the sacred animal again? The cat's complained of me?'

'I've gone too far,' thought Alain, as he closed the garage door. He crossed the street again and rejoined his wife who was waiting for him in battle order. 'Either I give in for the sake of a quiet night, or I stop the discussion by giving her a good, hard slap ... or ... It's too soon.'

'Well! I'm talking to you!'

'Let's go up first,' said Alain.

They did not speak as they went up, squeezed side by side in the narrow lift. As soon as they reached the studio, Camille tore off her béret and gloves and threw them across the room as if to show she had not given up the quarrel. Alain busied himself with Saha, inviting her to quit her perilous post. Patient, determined not to displease him, the cat followed him into the bathroom.

'If it's because of what you heard before dinner, when you came in,' began Camille shrilly the moment he reappeared.

Alain had decided on his line and interrupted her wearily: 'My dear, what are we going to say to each other? Nothing that we don't know already. That you can't bear the cat, that you blew up Mother Buque because the cat broke a vase – or a glass – I saw the pieces. I shall answer that I'm extremely fond of Saha and that you'd be just as jealous if I'd kept a warm affection for some friend of my childhood. And so it'll go on all night. I'd prefer to sleep, thanks very much. Look here, the next time, I advise you to take the initiative and have a little dog.'

Startled, embarrassed by having nothing for her temper to fasten on, Camille stared at him with raised eyebrows.

'The next time? What next time? What do you mean? What initiative?'

As Alain merely shrugged his shoulders, she flushed, her face suddenly became very young again and the extreme brightness of her eyes presaged tears. 'Oh, how bored I am!' groaned Alain inwardly. 'She's going to admit it. She's going to tell me I was right. How boring!'

'Listen, Alain.'

With an effort, he feigned anger and assumed a false air of authority.

'No, my dear. No, no, no! You're not going to force me to finish off this charming evening with a barren discussion. You're not going to make a drama out of a piece of childish nonsense any more than you're going to stop me being fond of animals.'

A kind of bitter gaiety came into Camille's eyes but she said nothing. 'Perhaps I was a little hard. "Childish nonsense," was unnecessary. And as to being fond of animals, what do I know about that?' A small, shadowy blue shape, outlined like a cloud with a hem of silver, sitting on the dizzy edge of the night, absorbed his thoughts and removed him from that soulless place where, inch by inch, he was defending his chance of solitude, his egotism, his poetry...

'Come along, my little enemy,' he said with disloyal charm, 'let's go and rest.'

She opened the door of the bathroom where Saha, installed for the night on the cork-seated stool, appeared to take only the faintest notice of her.

'But why, but why? Why did you say "the next time"?'

The noise of running water drowned Camille's voice. Alain did not attempt to answer. When he rejoined her in the huge bed, he wished her good-night and kissed her carelessly on her unpowdered nose, while Camille's mouth clung to his chin with a small greedy sound.

Waking early, he went off quietly to lie down on the 'waiting-room bench', the narrow divan squeezed between two walls of glass panes.

It was there that, during the following nights, he finished off his sleep. He closed the opaque oilcloth curtains on either side; they were almost new but already half destroyed by the sun. He breathed on his body the very perfume of his solitude, the sharp feline smell of restharrow and flowering box. One arm extended, the other folded on his chest, he resumed the relaxed, lordly attitude of his childhood sleep. Suspended from the narrow top of the three-cornered house, he encouraged with all his might the return of his old dreams which the lover's exhaustion had dispersed.

He escaped more easily than Camille could have wished, constrained as he was to fly on the very spot. Escape no longer meant a staircase descended on tiptoe, the slamming of a taxi door, a brief farewell note. None of his mistresses had prepared him for Camille and her young girl's eagerness; Camille and her reckless desire. Neither had they prepared him for Camille's stoical behaviour as an offended partner. She made it a point of honour not to complain.

Having escaped and lain down again on the waiting-room bench, Alain strained an uneasy ear toward the room he had just left, as his head felt for the hard little cushion he preferred to all the others. But Camille never reopened the door. Left alone, she pulled the crumpled sheet and the silk eiderdown over her, gnawed her bent finger in resentful regret, and snapped off the chromium strip-light which threw a narrow white beam across the bed. Alain never knew whether she had slept in the empty bed or whether she was learning so young that a solitary night imposes an armed vigil. It was impossible to tell, since she reappeared fresh and rather carefully dressed instead of in the bathrobe and pyjamas of the night before. But she could not understand that a man's sensuality is brief and seasonal and that its unpredictable return is never a new beginning.

Lying alone, bathed in the night air, measuring the height and the silence of his tower-top by the faintness of the hoots from the boats on the near-by Seine, the unfaithful husband delayed going to sleep till the apparition of Saha. She came to him, a shadow bluer than the shadows, along the ledge outside the open glass pane. There she stayed on the watch and would not come down on to Alain's chest although he implored her with the words that she knew: 'Come, my little puma, come along . . . My cat of the tree-tops, my cat of the lilacs. Saha, Saha, Saha.'

She resisted, sitting there above him on the window-sill. He could see nothing of her but her cat's shape against the sky, her chin down and her ears passionately orientated towards him. He could never catch the expression of her look.

Sometimes the dry dawn, the dawn before the wind got up, found the two of them sitting on the east side balcony. Cheek by cheek they watched the sky pale and the flight of white pigeons leaving the beautiful cedar of the Folie-Saint-James one by one. Together they felt the same surprise at being so high above the earth, so alone and so far from being happy. With the ardent, sinuous movement of a huntress, Saha followed the pigeons' flight and uttered an occasional 'ek . . . ek . . .' the faint echo of the 'mouek . . . mouek . . .' of excitement, greed, and violent games.

'Our room,' Alain said in her ear. 'Our garden, our house.'

She was getting thin again and Alain found her light and enchanting. But he suffered at seeing her so gentle and patient. Her patience was that of all those who are wearied out and sustained by a promise.

Sleep overcame Alain again as soon as daylight had begun to shorten the shadows. Rayless at first and looming larger through the mist of Paris, the sun swiftly shrank and

lightened. As it rose, already burning hot, it awoke a twit-
tering of sparrows in the gardens. The growing light revealed all the untidiness of a hot night on balconies and
window-sills and in little yards where captive shrubs
languished – a garment forgotten on a deck-chair, empty
glasses on a metal table, a pair of sandals. Alain hated the
indecency of small dwellings oppressed by summer and
regained his bed with one bound through a yawning panel
in the glass. At the foot of the nine-storeyed building, a
gardener lifted his head and saw this white young man
leap through the transparent wall like a burglar.

Saha did not follow him. Sometimes she strained her
ears in the direction of the triangular room; sometimes
she dispassionately watched the awakening of the distant
world on ground level. Someone let out a dog from a small
decrepit house. The dog leapt forward without a bark,
rushed round and round the tiny garden, and did not recover its voice until it had finished its aimless run. Women
appeared at the windows; a maid furiously slammed doors
and shook out orange cushions on a flat roof; men, waking
regretfully, lit the first bitter cigarette. At last, in the fire-
less kitchen of the Wedge, the automatic, whistling coffee-
pot and the electric teapot clashed against each other;
through the porthole window of the bathroom there
emerged Camille's perfume and her noisy yawning. Saha
resignedly folded her paws beneath her and pretended to
sleep.

EIGHT

ONE evening in July, when the two of them were waiting for Alain's return, Camille and the cat were resting on the same parapet; the cat crouched on all four paws, Camille leaning on her folded arms. Camille did not like this balcony-terrace, reserved for the cat and shut in by two cement partitions which cut off both the wind and all communication with the balcony on the prow.

They exchanged a glance of sheer mutual investigation and Camille did not say a word to Saha. Propped on her elbows, she leant over as if to count the storeys by the orange awnings that flapped from top to bottom of the dizzy façade, she brushed against the cat who got up to make room for her, stretched, and lay down a little farther off.

When Camille was alone, she looked very much like the little girl who did not want to say 'how d'you do?' Her face returned to childhood because it wore that expression of inhuman innocence, of angelic hardness which ennobles children's faces. Her gaze wandered over Paris, over the sky from which the light drained a little earlier each day, with an impartial severity which possibly condemned nothing. She yawned nervously, stood upright, and took a few absent-minded steps. Then she leant over again, forcing the cat to jump down. Saha stalked away with dignity and would have preferred to go back into the room. But the door in the hypotenuse had been shut and Saha patiently sat down. The next moment she had to get out of Camille's way for she was pacing from one partition to the other with long, jerky strides. The cat jumped back on to the parapet. As if in play, Camille dislodged her as she leant on her elbows and once again Saha took refuge against the closed door.

Motionless, her eyes far away, Camille stood with her back to her. Nevertheless the cat was looking at Camille's back and her breath came faster. She got up, turned two

or three times on her own axis and looked questioningly
at the closed door. Camille had not moved. Saha inflated
her nostrils and showed a distress which was almost like
nausea. A long, desolate mew escaped from her, the
wretched reply to a silent imminent threat. Camille faced
round abruptly.

She was a trifle pale; that is to say, her rouge stood out
in two oval moons on her cheeks. She affected an air of
absent-mindedness as she would if a human eye had been
staring at her. She even began to sing under her breath
and resumed her pacing from one partition to the other,
pacing to the rhythm of her song, but her voice failed her.
She forced the cat, whom her foot was about to kick, to
regain her narrow observation post with one bound, then
to flatten herself against the door.

Saha had regained her self-control and would have died
rather than utter a second cry. Tracking the cat down,
without appearing to see her, Camille paced to and fro in
silence. Saha did not jump on the parapet till Camille's feet
were right on top of her and she only leapt down again on to
the floor of the balcony to avoid the outstretched arm which
would have hurled her from the height of the nine storeys.

She fled methodically and jumped carefully, keeping her
eyes fixed on her adversary and condescending neither to
fury nor to supplication. The most violent emotion of all,
the terror of dying, soaked the sensitive soles of her paws
with sweat so that they left flower-like prints on the stucco
balcony.

Camille seemed the first to weaken and to lose her
criminal strength. She made the mistake of noticing that
the sun was going down, gave a glance at her wrist watch,
and was aware of the clink of glasses inside. A moment or
two more and her resolution would have deserted her as
sleep deserts the somnambulist, leaving her guiltless and
exhausted. Saha felt her enemy's firmness waver, hesitated
on the parapet and Camille, stretching out both arms,
pushed her into space.

She had time to hear the grating of claws on the rough-cast wall, to see Saha's blue body, twisted into an S, clutching the air with the force of a rising trout; then she shrank away, with her back to the wall.

She felt no temptation to look down into the little kitchen garden edged with new rubble. Back in the room, she put her hands over her ears, withdrew them, and shook her head as if she could hear the hum of a mosquito. Then she sat down and nearly fell asleep. But the oncoming night brought her to her feet again. She drove away the twilight by lighting up glass bricks, luminous tubes, and blinding mushrooms of lamps. She also lit up the long chromium eye which poured the opaline beam of its glance across the bed.

She walked about with supple movements, handling objects with light, adroit, dreaming hands.

'It's as if I'd got thinner,' she said out loud.

She changed her clothes and dressed herself in white.

'My fly in the milk,' she said, imitating Alain's voice. Her cheeks regained their colour at a sudden sensual memory which brought her back to reality and she waited for Alain's arrival.

She bent her head in the direction of the buzzing lift and shivered at every noise; those dull knockings, those metallic clangs, those sounds as of a boat grinding at anchor, those muffled bursts of music, which echo the discordant life of a new block of flats. But she was not surprised when the hollow tinkle of the bell in the hall replaced the fumbling of a key in the lock. She ran and opened the door herself.

'Shut the door,' Alain ordered. 'I must see first of all whether she hasn't hurt herself. Come and hold the lamp for me.'

He carried Saha alive in his arms. He went straight to the bedroom, pushed aside the things on the invisible dressing-table, and gently put the cat on the slab of glass. She held herself upright and firm on her paws but her deep-set eyes wandered all about her as they would have done in a strange house.

'Saha!' called Alain in a whisper. 'If there's nothing the matter with her, it's a miracle. Saha!'

She raised her head, as if to reassure her friend, and leant her cheek against his hand.

'Walk a little, Saha. Look, she's walking! Good Lord! Falling six storeys. It was the awning of the chap on the second floor that broke the fall. From there she bounced off on to the concierge's little lawn – the concierge saw her pass in the air. He said: "I thought it was an umbrella falling." What's she got on her ear? No, it's some white off the wall. Wait till I listen to her heart.'

He laid the cat on her side and listened to the beating ribs, the tiny disordered mechanism. With his fair hair spread out and his eyes closed, he seemed to be sleeping on Saha's flank and to wake with a sigh only to see Camille standing there silent and apart, watching the close-knit group they made.

'Can you believe it? There's nothing wrong. At least I can't find anything wrong with her except a terribly agitated heart. But a cat's heart is usually agitated. But however could it have happened! I'm asking you as if you could possibly know, my poor pet! She fell from this side,' he said, looking at the open french window. 'Jump down on the ground, Saha, if you can.'

After hesitating, she jumped but lay down again on the carpet. She was breathing fast and went on looking all round the room with the same uncertain look.

'I think I'll phone Chéron. Still, look, she's washing herself. She wouldn't wash herself if she'd been injured internally. Oh, good Lord!'

He stretched, threw his jacket on the bed, and came over to Camille.

'What a fright. How pretty you look, all in white. Kiss me, my fly in the milk!'

She let herself fall into the arms which had remembered her at last and could not hold back some broken sobs.

'No? You're actually crying?'

He was upset himself and hid his forehead in the soft, black hair.

'I . . . I didn't know that you were kind.'

She had the courage not to draw away from him at that. However, Alain quickly returned to Saha whom he wanted to take out on the balcony because of the heat. But the cat resisted and contented herself with lying near the open door, turned towards the evening, blue as herself. From time to time, she gave a brief shudder and looked anxiously into the triangular room behind her.

'It's the shock,' explained Alain. 'I wanted her to go and sit outside.'

'Leave her alone,' said Camille faintly, 'since she doesn't want to.'

'Her wishes are orders. Today, of all days! Is there likely to be anything eatable left over at this hour? It's half-past nine!'

Mother Buque wheeled the table out on to the balcony and they dined looking over the east side of Paris where the most lights glimmered. Alain talked a lot, drank water with a little wine in it, and accused Saha of clumsiness, impudence, and 'cat's sins'.

' "Cat's sins" are the kind of playful mistakes and lapses of judgement which can be put down to their having been civilized and domesticated. They've nothing in common with the clumsiness and carelessness that are almost deliberate.'

But Camille no longer asked him: 'How do you know that?' After dinner, he carried Saha and drew Camille into the studio where the cat consented to drink the milk she had refused. As she drank, she shivered all over as cats do when they are given something too cold to drink.

'It's the shock,' Alain repeated. 'All the same, I shall ask Chéron to look in and see her tomorrow morning. Oh, I'm forgetting everything!' he cried gaily. 'Will you phone the concierge? I've left that roll of plans down in his lodge. The one that Massart, our precious furnishing chap, deposited there.'

Camille obeyed while Alain, tired and relaxed after the strain, dropped into one of the scattered armchairs and closed his eyes.

'Hallo!' said Camille at the telephone. 'Yes... That must be it. A big roll ... Thanks so much'

He laughed with his eyes still closed. She had returned to his side and stood there, watching him laugh.

'That absurd little voice you put on! What is this new little voice? "A big roll ... Thanks so much",' he mimicked. 'Do you keep that extremely small voice for the concierge? Come here, it needs the two of us to face Massart's latest creations.'

He unrolled a sheet of thick drawing-paper, on the ebony table. Saha, who loved all kinds of paper, promptly leapt on the tinted drawing.

'Isn't she sweet!' exclaimed Alain. 'It's to show me she's not in the least hurt. O my miraculously escaped one! Hasn't she a bump on her head? Camille, feel her head. No, she hasn't a bump. Feel her head all the same, Camille.'

A poor little murderess meekly tried to emerge from her banishment, stretched out her hand, and touched the cat's head with humble hatred.

Her gesture was received with the most savage snarl, a scream, and an epileptic leap. Camille shrieked 'Ha!' as if she had been burned. Standing on the unrolled drawing the cat covered the young woman with a flaming stare of accusation, the fur on her back erect, her teeth bared, and the dry red of her open jaw showing.

Alain had sprang up, ready to protect Saha and Camille from each other.

'Take care! She's ... perhaps she's mad ... Saha!'

She stared at him angrily but with a lucidity that proved she had not lost her reason.

'What happened? Where did you touch her?'

'I didn't touch her at all.'

They were both speaking low, hardly moving their lips.

'Then, why this?' said Alain. 'I don't understand. Put your hand out again.'

'No, I don't want to!' protested Camille. 'Perhaps she's gone wild,' she added.

Alain took the risk of stroking Saha. She flattened her erect fur and yielded to the friendly palm but glared once more at Camille with brilliant, accusing eyes.

'Why *this*?' Alain repeated slowly. 'Look, she's got a scratch on her nose. I hadn't seen it. It's dried blood. Saha, Saha, good now,' he said, seeing the fury growing in the yellow eyes.

Because her cheeks were swelled out and her whiskers stiffly thrust forward as if she were hunting, the furious cat seemed to be laughing. The joy of battle stretched the mauve corners of her mouth and tautened the mobile, muscular chin. The whole of her feline face was striving towards a universal language, towards a word forgotten by men.

'Whatever's *that*?' said Alain suddenly.

'Whatever's *what*?'

Under the cat's stare Camille was recovering her courage and the instinct of self-defence. Leaning over the drawing, Alain could make out damp prints in groups of four little spots round a central, irregular patch.

'Her paws . . . wet?' muttered Alain.

'She must have walked in some water,' said Camille. 'You're making a fuss about nothing.'

Alain raised her head towards the dry blue night.

'In water? What water?'

He turned again to his wife. He looked at her with round eyes which made him look suddenly extraordinarily ugly.

'Don't you know what those footprints mean?' he said harshly. 'No, *you* wouldn't know. Fear, d'you understand, *fear*. The sweat of fear. Cat's sweat, the only time cats *do* sweat. So she was frightened.'

Delicately, he lifted one of Saha's front paws and dried the sweat on the fleshy pad. Then he pulled back the living white sheath into which the claws had been drawn back.

'She's got all her claws broken,' he said, talking to himself. 'She must have held on ... clutching. She scratched the stone trying to save herself. She ...'

He broke off his monologue and, without another word, took the cat under his arm and carried her off to the bathroom

Alone, unmoving, Camille strained her ears. She kept her hands knotted together; free as she was, she seemed to be loaded with fetters.

'Madame Buque,' said Alain's voice, 'have you any milk?'

'Yes, Monsieur. In the 'fridge.'

'Then it's ice-cold?'

'But I can warm it on the stove. It won't take a second. It is for the cat? She's not ill, is she?'

'No, she's ...'

Alain's voice stopped short and changed its tone: 'She's a little off meat in this heat. Thank you, Madame Buque. Yes, you can go now. See you in the morning.'

Camille heard her husband moving to and fro and turning on a tap. She knew that he was giving the cat food and fresh water. A diffused shadow, above the metal lampshade, came up as high as her face which was as still as a mask except for the slow movement of the great eyes.

Alain returned, carelessly tightening his leather belt, and sat down again at the ebony table. But he did not summon Camille back to sit beside him and she was forced to speak first.

'You've sent old Mother Buque off?'

'Yes. Shouldn't I have?'

He lit a cigarette and squinted at the flame of the lighter. 'I wanted her to bring something tomorrow morning.'

'Oh, it doesn't matter a bit ... don't apologize.'

'But I'm not apologizing. Though, actually, I ought to.'

He went over to the open bay window, drawn by the blue of the night. He was studying a certain tremor in himself, a tremor which did not come from his recent emotion, but which was more like the tremolo of an orchestra, muffled and foreboding. From the Folie-Saint-James a rocket shot up, burst into luminous petals that withered one by one as they fell, and the blue of the night recovered its peace and its powdery depth. In the amusement park, a grotto, a colonnade, and a waterfall were suddenly lit up with incandescent white; Camille came nearer to him.

'Are they having a gala night? Let's wait for the fireworks. Do you hear the guitars?'

Absorbed in his inner tremor, he did not answer her. His wrists and hands were tingling, his loins were weak and felt as if a thousand insects were crawling over them. His state reminded him of the hateful lassitude, the fatigue he used to feel after the school sports. After running and rowing he would emerge vindictive, throbbing and exhausted and equally contemptuous of his victory or defeat. Now, he was at peace only in that part of himself which was no longer anxious about Saha. For several minutes – or perhaps for very few – ever since the discovery of the broken claws, ever since Saha's furious terror, he had lost all sense of time.

'It's not fireworks,' he said. 'Probably just some dances.'

From the movement Camille made beside him in the shadow, he realized that she had given up expecting him to answer her. He felt her coming closer without apprehension. He saw the outline of the white dress; a bare arm; a half face lit by the yellow light from the lamps indoors and a half face that shadowed blue in the clear night. The two halves were divided by the small straight nose and each was provided with a large, almost unblinking eye.

'Yes, of course, it's dances,' she agreed. 'They're mandolines, not guitars. Listen... "*Les donneurs... de sé-é-réna ... des, Et les bel-les é-écou-teu ...*'

Her voice cracked on the highest note and she coughed to excuse her failure.

'But what a tiny voice...' thought Alain, astonished. 'What has she done with her voice that's as big and open as her eyes? She's singing in a little girl's voice. Hoarse, too.'

The mandolines stopped and the breeze brought a faint

human noise of clapping and applause. A moment later, a rocket shot up, burst into an umbrella of mauve rays in which hung tears of living fire.

'Oh!' cried Camille.

Both of them had emerged from the darkness like two statues; Camille in lilac marble; Alain whiter, with his hair greenish and his eyes almost colourless. When the rocket had gone out, Camille sighed.

'It never lasts long enough,' she said plaintively.

The distant music started again. But the capricious wind deadened the sound of the stringed instruments into a vague shrill buzzing and carried the blasts of the accompanying brass, on two notes, loudly and insistently right into their ears.

'What a shame,' said Camille. 'They've probably got a frightfully good jazz band. That's *Love in the Night* they're playing.'

She hummed the tune in a high, shaky, almost inaudible voice, as if she had just been crying. This new voice of hers acutely increased Alain's disquiet. It induced in him a need for revelation, a desire to break down whatever it was that – a long time ago or only a moment ago? – had risen between himself and Camille. It was something to which he could not yet give a name but which was growing fast; something which prevented him from putting his arm round her neck like a boy; something which kept him motionless at her side, alert and expectant, against the wall still warm from the heat of the day. Turning impatient, he said, 'Go on singing.'

A long red, white, and blue shower, falling like the branches of a weeping willow, streaked the sky over the park and showed Alain a Camille startled and already defiant: 'Singing what?'

'*Love in the Night* or anything else. It doesn't matter what.'

She hesitated, then refused.

'Let me listen to the jazz . . . even from here you can hear it's simply marvellous.'

He did not insist. He restrained his impatience and mastered the tingling which had now spread over his entire body.

A swarm of gay little suns, revolving brightly against the darkness, took flight. Alain secretly confronted them with the constellations of his favourite dreams.

'Those are the ones to remember. I'll try and take them with me down there,' he noted gravely. 'I've neglected my dreams too much.' At last, in the sky over the Folie, there rose and expanded a kind of straying pink and yellow dawn which burst into vermilion discs and fiery ferns and ribbons of blinding metal.

The shouts of children on the lower balconies greeted this miraculous display. By its light, Alain saw Camille absent and remote, absorbed in other lights in her own mind.

As soon as the night closed in again, his hesitation vanished and he slipped his own bare arm under Camille's. As he touched that bare arm, he fancied he could see it; its whiteness hardly tinged by the summer and clothed in a fine down that lay flat on the skin, reddish-brown on the forearm, paler near the shoulder.

'You're cold,' he murmured. 'You're not feeling ill?'

She began to cry very quietly and so promptly that Alain suspected she had been preparing her tears.

'No. It's you. It's you who . . . who don't love me.'

He leant back against the wall and drew Camille against his hip. He could feel her trembling, and cold from her shoulders to her knees, bare above her rolled stockings. She clung to him faithfully, leaning all her weight on him.

'Aha, so I don't love you. Right! Is this another jealousy scene on account of Saha?'

He felt a muscular tremor run through the whole of the body he was supporting, a renewal of energy and self-defence. Encouraged by the moment, by a kind of indescribable opportunism, he insisted: 'Instead of adopting this charming animal, like me. Are we the only young couple who have a cat or a dog? Would you like a parrot or a marmoset – a pair of doves – a dog, to make me very jealous in my turn?'

She shook her shoulders, protesting with annoyance through closed lips. With his head high, Alain carefully controlled his own voice and egged himself on. 'Go on, a few more bits of nonsense; fill her up and we'll get somewhere. She's like a jar that I've got to turn upside down to empty. Go on. Go on.'

'Would you like a little lion . . . or a baby crocodile of barely fifty? No? Come on, you'd much better adopt Saha. If you'd just take the least bit of trouble, you'd soon see . . .'

Camille wrenched herself out of his arms so violently that he staggered.

'No!' she cried. '*That*, never! Do you hear me? *Never!*'

'Ah, now we've got it!' Alain said to himself with delight. He pushed Camille into the room, pulled down the outer blind, lit up the rectangle of glass in the ceiling, and shut the window. With an animal movement, Camille rushed over to the window and Alain opened it again.

'On condition you don't scream,' he said.

He wheeled the only armchair up to Camille and sat astride on the solitary chair at the foot of the wide, turned-down bed with its new, clean sheets. The oilcloth curtains, drawn for the night, gave a greenish cast to Camille's pale face and her creased white dress.

'Well?' began Alain. 'No compromise possible? Appalling story? Either her or me?'

She answered with a brief nod and Alain realized that he must drop his bantering tone.

'What do you want me to say?' he went on, after a silence. 'The only thing I don't want to say to you? You know very well I'll never give up this cat. I should be ashamed to. Ashamed in myself and ashamed before her.'

'I know,' said Camille.

'And before you,' Alan finished.

'Oh, *me*!' said Camille, raising her hand.

'You count too,' said Alain hardly. 'Tell me. Is it only me

you've anything against? You've no reproach against Saha except her affection for me?'

She answered only with a troubled, hesitant look and he was irritated at having to go on questioning her. He had thought that a short violent scene would force all the issues; he had relied on this easy way out. But, after her one cry, Camille had stiffened defensively and was furnishing no fuel for a quarrel. He resorted to patience: 'Tell me, my dear. What is it? Mustn't I call you my dear? Tell me, if it were a question of another cat and not Saha, would you be so intolerant?'

'Of course I wouldn't,' she said very quickly. 'You wouldn't love it as much as that one.'

'Quite true,' said Alain with loyal accuracy.

'Even a woman,' went on Camille, beginning to get heated, 'you probably wouldn't love a *woman* as much as that.'

'Quite true,' said Alain.

'You're not like most people who are fond of animals. No, you're *not*. Patrick's fond of animals. He takes big dogs by the scruff of their necks and rolls them over. He imitates cats to see the faces they make – he whistles to the birds.'

'Quite. In other words, he's not difficult,' said Alain.

'But you're quite different. You *love* Saha.'

'I've never pretended not to. But I wasn't lying to you, either, when I said to you: "Saha's not your rival." '

He broke off and lowered his eyelids over his secret which was a secret of purity.

'There are rivals *and* rivals,' said Camille sarcastically.

Suddenly she reddened. Flushed with sudden intoxication, she advanced to Alain.

'I saw the two of you!' she almost shrieked. 'In the morning, when you spend the night on your little divan. Before daybreak. I've seen you, both of you.'

She pointed a shaking hand towards the balcony.

'Sitting there, the two of you ... you didn't even hear me! You were like that, cheek to cheek.'

She went over to the window, recovered her breath and marched down on Alain again.

'It's for you to say honestly whether I'm wrong in being jealous of this cat and wrong in suffering.'

He kept silence so long that she became angry again.

'Do speak! Do *say* something! At the point we've got to ... What are you waiting for?'

'The sequel,' said Alain. 'The rest.'

He stood up quietly, bent over his wife, and lowered his voice as he indicated the french window: 'It was you, wasn't it? You threw her over?'

With a swift movement she put the bed between herself and him but she did not deny it. He watched her escape with a kind of smile: 'You threw her over,' he said dreamily. 'I felt very definitely that you'd changed everything between us. You threw her over ... she broke her claws trying to clutch on to the wall.'

He lowered his head, imagining the attempted murder.

'But *how* did you throw her over? By holding her by the skin of her neck? By taking advantage of her being asleep on the parapet? Had you been planning this for a long time? You hadn't had a fight with each other first?'

He raised his head and stared at Camille's hands and arms.

'No, you've no marks. She accused you well and truly, didn't she, when I made you touch her. She was magnificent.'

His eyes left Camille and embraced the night, the dust of stars, the tops of the three poplars which the lights in the room lit up.

'Very well,' he said simply, 'I'm going away.'

'Oh listen ... do *listen* ...' Camille implored wildly, almost in a whisper.

Nevertheless, she let him go out of the room. He opened cupboards, talked to the cat in the bathroom. The sound of his footsteps warned Camille that he had changed into his outdoor shoes and she looked, automatically, at the time. He came in again, carrying Saha in a bulging basket which Mme Buque used for shopping. Hurriedly dressed, with his hair dishevelled and a scarf round his neck, his untidiness so much suggested that of a lover that Camille's eyelids pricked. But she heard Saha moving in the basket and tightened her lips.

'As you see, I'm going away,' repeated Alain. He lowered his eyes, lifted the basket a trifle, and corrected himself with calculated cruelty. '*We're* going away.'

He secured the wicker lid, explaining as he did so: 'This was all I could find in the kitchen.'

'You're going to your home?' inquired Camille, forcing herself to imitate Alain's calm.

'But of course.'

'Are you ... can I count on seeing you during the next few days?'

'Why, certainly.'

Surprise made her weaken again. She had to make an immense effort not to plead, not to weep.

'What about you?' said Alain. 'Will you stay here alone tonight? You won't be frightened? If you insisted, I'd stay, but ...'

He turned his head towards the balcony.

'But, frankly, I'm not keen on it. What do you propose to say to your family?'

Hurt at his sending her, by implication, home to her people, Camille pulled herself together.

'I've nothing to say to them. These are things which only concern *me*, I presume. I've no inclination for family councils.'

'I entirely agree with you ... provisionally.'

'Anyway, we can decide as from tomorrow.'

He raised his free hand to ward off this threat of a future.

'No. Not tomorrow. Today there isn't any tomorrow.'

In the doorway, he turned back.

'In the bathroom, you'll find my key and all the money we've got here.'

She interrupted with irony: 'Why not a hamper of provisions and a compass?'

She was putting on a brave act and surveyed him with one hand on her hip and her head erect on her handsome neck. 'She's building up my exit,' thought Alain. He wanted to reply with some similar last-minute coquetry, to toss his hair over his forehead and give her that narrowed look between his lashes which seemed to disdain what it rested on. But he renounced a pantomime which would look absurd when he was carrying a shopping-basket and confined himself to a vague bow in Camille's direction.

She kept up her expression of bravado and her theatrical stance. But before he went out, he could see more clearly, at a distance, the dark circles round her eyes and the moisture which covered her temples and her smooth, unlined neck.

Downstairs, he crossed the street automatically, the key of the garage in his hand. 'I can't do that,' he thought and he retraced his steps towards the avenue some way off where cruising taxis could be picked up at night. Saha mewed two or three times and he calmed her with his voice. 'I can't do that. But it really would be much pleasanter to take the car. Neuilly is impossible at night.' He was surprised, having counted on a blessed sense of release, to find himself losing his composure as soon as he was alone. Walking did not restore his calm. When, at last, he found a stray taxi, the five-minute drive seemed almost interminable.

He shivered in the warm night under the gas-jet, waiting for the gate to be opened. Saha, who had recognized the smell of the garden, was giving short sharp mews in the basket which he had put down on the pavement.

The scent of the wistarias in their second flowering came across the air and Alain shivered more violently, stamping from one foot to the other as if it were bitterly cold. He rang again but the house gave no sign of life in spite of the solemn, scandalous clamour of the big bell. At last a light appeared in the little buildings by the garage and he heard old Émile's dragging feet on the gravel.

'It's me, Émile,' he said when the colourless face of the old valet peered through the bars.

'Monsieur Alain?' said Émile, exaggerating his quavering voice. 'Monsieur Alain's young lady isn't indisposed? The summer is so treacherous. Monsieur Alain has some luggage, I see.'

'No, it's Saha. Leave her, I'll carry her. No, don't turn up the gas-lamps, the light might wake Madame. Just open the front door for me and go back to bed.'

'Madame is awake – it was she who rang for me. I hadn't heard the big bell. In my first sleep, you see.'

Alain hurried ahead to escape Émile's chatter and the sound of his shaky footsteps following him. He did not stumble at the turnings of the paths though there was no moon that night. The great lawn, paler than the flower-beds, guided him. The dead, draped tree in the middle of the grass looked like a huge standing man with his coat over his arm. The smell of watered geraniums made Alain's throat tighten and he stopped. He bent down, opened the basket with groping fingers, and released the cat.

'Saha, our garden.'

He felt her glide out of the basket and, from pure tenderness, took no more notice of her. Like an offering, he gave her back the night, her liberty, the soft spongy earth, the wakeful insects, and the sleeping birds.

Behind the shutters on the ground floor, a lighted lamp was waiting and Alain's spirits fell again. 'To have to talk again, to have to explain to my mother . . . explain what? It's so simple. It's so difficult.'

All he longed for was silence, the room with the faded flowers on the wallpaper, his bed, and, above all, for vehement tears; great sobs as raucous as coughs that would be his secret, guilty compensation.

'Come in, darling, come in.'

He seldom went into his mother's room. His selfish aversion to medicine bottles and droppers, boxes of digitalis pills and homoeopathic remedies dated from childhood and was as acute as ever. But he could not resist the sight

of the narrow, unadorned bed and of the woman with the
thick white hair who was heaving herself up on her
wrists.

'You know, Mother, there's nothing extraordinary about
all this.'

He accompanied this idiotic statement with a smile of
which he was promptly ashamed; a horizontal, stiff-cheeked
smile. His tiredness had overwhelmed him in the sudden
rush, making him do and say the exact opposite of what he
meant to. He sat down by his mother's bedside and
loosened his scarf.

'Forgive my appearance. I came just as I was. I arrive at
preposterous times without giving you warning.'

'But you did give me warning,' said Mme Amparat.

She glanced at Alain's dusty shoes.

'Your shoes look like a tramp's.'

'I've only come from my place, Mother. But it was a long
time before I could find a taxi. I was carrying the cat.'

'Ah,' said Mme Amparat, with an understanding look.
'You've brought back the cat?'

'Yes, of course. If you knew . . .'

He stopped, restrained by an odd discretion. 'These are
things one doesn't tell. These stories aren't for parents.'

'Camille's not very fond of Saha, Mother.'

'I know,' said Mme Amparat.

She forced herself to smile and shook her wavy hair.

'That's extremely serious!'

'Yes. For Camille,' said Alain spitefully.

He got up and paced about among the furniture. It had
white covers on it for the summer like the furniture in
houses in the provinces. Having made up his mind not to
denounce Camille, he could find nothing more to say.

'You know, Mother, there haven't been any screams or
smashing of crockery. The glass dressing-table's still intact
and the neighbours haven't come rushing up. Only I just
need a little . . . a little time to be by myself . . . to rest. I
won't hide it from you. I'm at the end of my tether,' he
said, seating himself on the bed.

'No. You don't hide it from me,' said Mme Amparat. She laid a hand on Alain's forehead, turning up the young face, on which the pale stubble was beginning to show, towards the light. He complained, turning his changeable eyes away, and succeeded in holding off a little longer the storm of tears he had promised himself.

'If there aren't any sheets on my old bed, Mother, I'll wrap myself up in any old thing.'

'There are sheets on your bed,' said Mme Amparat.

At that, he threw his arms round his mother and kissed her blindly on her eyes and cheeks and hair. He thrust his face into her neck, stammered 'Good-night' and went out of the room, sniffing.

In the hall, he pulled himself together and did not go upstairs at once. The night which was ending called to him and so did Saha. But he did not go far. The steps down into the garden were far enough. He sat down on one of them in the darkness and his outstretched hand encountered the fur, the sensitive antennae-like whiskers, and the cool nostrils of Saha.

She turned round and round on one spot according to the ritual of wild creatures when they caress. She seemed very small to him and light as a kitten. Because he was hungry himself, he thought she must be needing food.

"We'll eat tomorrow . . . quite soon now . . . it's almost daylight.'

Already she smelt of mint and geranium and box. He held her there, trusting and perishable, promised, perhaps, ten years of life. And he suffered at the thought of the briefness of so great a love.

'After you, probably anyone can have me who wants me. A woman, many women. But never another cat.'

A blackbird whistled four notes that rang through the whole garden. But the sparrows had heard it and answered. On the lawn and the massed flowerbeds, faint ghosts of colour began to appear. Alain could make out a sickly white, a dull red more melancholy than black itself, a yellow smeared on the surrounding green, a round yellow flower which began to revolve and become more yellow and was followed by eyes and moons. Staggering, dropping with sleep, Alain reached his room, threw off his clothes, uncovered the bed, and was unconscious almost as soon as he had slipped between the cool sheets.

Lying on his back with one arm flung out and the cat, silent and concentrated, kneading his shoulder, he was falling straight like a plummet into the very depths of sleep when a start brought him back to the daylight, the swaying of the awakened trees, and the blessed clanging of the distant trams.

'What's the matter with me? I wanted ... Ah, yes! I wanted to cry.' He smiled and fell asleep again.

His sleep was feverish and crowded with dreams. Two or three times he thought he had woken up and was becoming conscious of where he was, but each time he was undeceived by the expression of the walls of his room. They were angrily watching the fluttering of a winged eye.

'But I'm asleep ... of course, I'm asleep.'

'I'm asleep ...' he answered again to the crunching gravel. 'I'm asleep, I tell you,' he called to two dragging feet that brushed against the door. The feet went away and the sleeper congratulated himself in his dream. But the dream had come to a head under the repeated solicitings and Alain opened his eyes.

The sun he had left on the window-sill in May had become an August sun and reached no farther than the satiny trunk of the tulip-tree opposite the house. 'How the summer has aged,' Alain said to himself. He got up, naked, looked for something to wear and found some pyjamas, too short and too tight in the sleeves and a faded dressing-gown which he joyfully pulled on. The window summoned him but he was stopped by Camille's photograph which he had left, forgotten, by his bed. Curiously, he examined the inaccurate, retouched little portrait; whitened here, blackened there. 'It's more like her than I supposed,' he thought. 'How was it I didn't notice it? Four months ago I used to say "Oh, she's entirely different from that. Much more subtle, not nearly so hard." But I was wrong.'

The long, steady breeze ran through the trees with a murmur like a river's. Dazed and quite painfully hungry, Alain lay back on his pillows. 'How delightful it is, a convalescence.' To complete the illusion a knuckle tapped on the door and the bearded Basque woman entered, carrying a tray.

'But I'd have had breakfast in the garden, Juliette!'

A kind of smile appeared among the grey hairs on her face.

'I thought as much. Would Monsieur Alain like me to take the tray down?'

'No, no, I'm too hungry. Leave that there. Saha'll come in by the window.'

He called the cat who rose from some invisible retreat as if she had come into existence at his call. She bounded up the vertical path of climbing plants and fell back again – she had forgotten her broken claws.

'Wait, I'm coming!'

He brought her back in his arms and they gorged themselves, she on milk and rusks, he on slices of bread and butter and scalding hot coffee. On one corner of the tray, a little rose adorned the lid of the honey-pot.

'It's not one of my mother's roses,' Alain decided. It was an ill-made, stunted little rose, picked from a low branch, that gave out the queer smell of a yellow rose. 'It's a little homage from the Basque.'

Saha, radiant, seemed to have grown plumper over-night. Her shirt-frill erect, her four darker stripes well marked between her ears, she stared at the garden with the eyes of a happy despot.

'How simple it all is, isn't it, Saha? For you, at any rate.'

Old Émile entered in his turn and insisted on removing Alain's shoes.

'There's one of the laces got very worn. Monsieur Alain hasn't another? It doesn't matter, I'll put one of my own laces in,' he bleated with emotion.

'Decidedly, it's my gala-day,' said Alain to himself. The word drove him back by contrast to all the things that only yesterday had been daily bothers; time to get up and dress, time to go to the Amparat office, time to come back to lunch with Camille.

'But I've nothing on earth to put on!' he cried.

In the bathroom he recognized the slightly rusty razor, the worn cake of pink soap, and the old toothbrush and used them with a delight of a man who has got shipwrecked for fun. But he had to come down in the outgrown pyjamas as the Basque woman had carried off his clothes.

'Come Saha, Saha.'

She went ahead and he ran after her uncertainly in a pair of frayed raffia sandals that kept threatening to slip off. He stretched out his shoulders to feel the cape of the mild sun fall on them and half closed his eyes that had grown unaccustomed to the green reverberations of the lawns and the hot colours which blazed above a serried block of crimson love-lies-bleeding and a tuft of red salvias bordered with heliotrope.

'Oh, the same, the very same salvias!'

Alain had always known that little heart-shaped bed as red and invariably bordered with heliotropes. It was shaded by a lean, ancient cherry-tree which occasionally produced a few cherries in September.

'I can see six ... seven. Seven green cherries!'

He was talking to the cat who, with empty, golden eyes, had her mouth half open, almost overcome by the excessive scent of the heliotropes. Her face had the look of almost sickened ecstasy animals assume when confronted with an overpowering smell.

She ate a blade of grass to recover herself, listened to various voices, and rubbed her nose against the hard twigs of the privet hedge. But she did not display any exuberance, any irresponsible gaiety and she walked nobly, surrounded by the tiny silver halo which outlined all her body.

'Thrown, from a height of nine storeys,' Alain thought as he watched her. 'Grabbed ... or pushed. Perhaps she defended herself ... perhaps she escaped to be caught again and thrown over. Assassinated.'

He tried by such conjectures to arouse his just anger, but he did not succeed. 'If I truly, deeply loved Camille, how furious I should be.' Around him shone his kingdom, threatened like all kingdoms. 'My mother assures me that in less than twenty years no one will be able to keep on houses and gardens like this. She's probably right. I'm quite willing to lose them. I don't want to let *them* come into them.'

He was shaken by the sound of a telephone ringing in the house. 'Come, come now! I'm not frightened, am I? Camille's not so stupid as to telephone me. To do her justice, I've never known a young woman so restrained in using that instrument.'

But he could not stop himself from running awkwardly towards the house, losing his sandals and tripping over pebbles, and calling out: 'Mother! Who's that on the phone?'

The thick white dressing-gown appeared on the steps and Alain felt ashamed of having called out.

'How I love your big white dressing-gown, Mother! Always the same, always the same.'

'Thank you very much on behalf of my dressing-gown,' said Mme Amparat.

She kept Alain waiting a moment before she said: 'It was Monsieur Veuillet. It's half-past nine. Have you forgotten the ways of the house?'

She combed her son's hair with her fingers and buttoned up the too-tight pyjamas jacket.

'You're a pretty sight. I suppose you don't intend to spend the rest of your life as a ragamuffin?'

Alain was grateful to her for questioning him so adroitly.

'No question of that, Mother. In a moment, I'll get busy about all that.'

Mme Amparat tenderly interrupted his vague, wide gesture.

'Tonight ... where will you be?'

'Here!' he cried, and the tears welled up in his eyes.

'Good gracious, what a child!' said Mme Amparat and he took up the word with the earnestness of a boy scout.

'Perhaps I am a child, Mother. That's why I want to think over what I ought to do to get out of this childishness.'

'Get out of it how? By a divorce? That's a door that makes a lot of noise.'

'But which lets in some air,' he dared to retort sharply.

'Wouldn't a separation ... a temporary one, give just as good results? What about a thorough rest or a little travel, perhaps?'

He threw up his arms indignantly.

'My poor dear Mother, you've no idea. You're a thousand miles from imagining.'

He was going to bring it all out and tell her about the attempted murder.

'Very well then, leave me a thousand miles! Such things don't concern me. Have a little ... a little reserve,' said Mme Amparat hastily and Alain took advantage of a misunderstanding which was due to her innate modesty.

'Now, Mother, there's still all the tiresome side to be thought of. I mean the family point of view which is all mixed up with the business side. From the Malmerts' point of view, my divorce will be quite indefensible, no matter how much Camille may be partly responsible. A bride of three and a half months! I can hear it all.'

'Where do you get the idea that there's a business side involved? You and the little Malmert girl aren't running a firm together. A married couple is not a pair of business partners.'

'I know, Mother. But if things turn out as I expect, there's bound to be a horrible period of formalities and interviews and so on. It's never as simple as everyone says, a divorce.'

She listened to her son with gentle forbearance. She knew that certain causes produce unexpected results and that, all through his life, a man has to be born many times with no other assistance than that of chance, of bruises, of mistakes.

'It's never simple to leave anything we've wanted to attach to ourselves,' said Mme Amparat. 'She's not so bad, that little Malmert. A little ... coarse, a little lacking in manners. No, not so bad. At least, that's my way of seeing it. I don't want to impose it on you. We've plenty of time to think it over.'

'I've taken care of that,' said Alain with harsh politeness. 'And, at the moment, I prefer to keep a certain story to myself.'

His face suddenly lit up in a laugh that restored it to childhood. Standing up on her hind legs, Saha, using her paw as a spoon, was fishing drowned ants out of a brimming watering-can.

'Look at her, Mother! Isn't she a miraculous cat?'

'Yes,' sighed Mme Amparat. 'She's your chimera.'

He was always surprised when his mother employed an unusual word. He greeted this one with a kiss on her prematurely aged hand with its swollen veins and the little brown flecks which Juliette lugubriously called 'earth-stains'.

At the sound of the bell ringing at the gate, he jerked himself upright.

'Run and hide,' said Mme Amparat. 'We're right in the way of the tradesmen. Go and dress yourself. Do you want the butcher's little boy to catch you in that extraordinary get-up?'

But they both knew perfectly well that it was not the butcher's little boy ringing at the visitor's gate. Mme Amparat had already turned her back and was hurrying up the steps, holding up her dressing-gown in both hands. Behind the clipped hedge Alain could see the Basque woman retreating in disorder, her black silk apron flying in the wind, while a slither of slippers on the gravel announced the flight of old Émile. Alain cut off his escape.

'You have at least opened the gate?'

'Yes, Monsieur Alain. The young lady's behind her car.'

He lifted terrified eyes to the sky, hunched up his shoulders, as if he were in a hailstorm, and vanished.

'Well, that's certainly something like a picnic! I wish I'd had time to get dressed. Gracious, she's got a new suit!'

Camille had seen him and came straight up to him without overmuch haste. In one of those moments of almost hilarious anxiety that crop up on dramatic occasions, he thought confusedly: 'Perhaps she's come to lunch.'

Carefully and lightly made-up as she was, armed with black lashes and beautiful parted lips and shining teeth, she seemed all the same to lose her self-assurance when Alain came forward to meet her. For he was approaching without breaking away from the shelter of his protective atmosphere. He was treading his native lawn under the rich patronage of the trees, and Camille looked at him with the eyes of a poor person.

'Forgive me, I look like a schoolboy who's suddenly shot up out of all knowledge. We didn't arrange to meet this morning, did we?'

'No. I've brought you your big suitcase. It's packed full.'

'But you shouldn't have done that!' he expostulated. 'I'd have sent Émile round today to fetch it.'

'Don't talk to me about Émile. I wanted to give him your case but the old idiot rushed off as if I'd got the plague. The case is down there by the gate.'

She flushed with humiliation, biting the inside of her cheek. 'It's beginning well,' said Alain to himself.

'I'm terribly sorry. You know what Émile's like. Listen,' he decided, 'let's go on the lawn inside the yew hedges. We'll be quieter there than in the house.'

He promptly repented his choice for that clearing, enclosed in clipped yews and furnished with wicker chairs, had been the scene of their secret kisses in the old days.

'Wait while I dust the twigs off. You mustn't spoil the pretty suit. Incidentally, I don't know it, do I?'

'It's new,' said Camille in a tone of profound sadness, as if she had said: 'It's dead.'

She sat sideways, looking about her. Two arched arcades,

one opposite the other, broke the circle of greenery. Alain
remembered something Camille had once confided to him:
'You've no idea how your beautiful garden used to frighten
me. I used to come here like the little girl from the village
who comes to play with the son of the grand people at the
château, in their park. And yet, when you come to think of
it . . .' She had spoiled everything by that last remark. That
'when you come to think of it' implied the prosperity of
Malmert Mangles compared with the declining house of
Amparat.

He observed that Camille kept her gloves on. 'That's a
precaution that defeats its own ends. Without those gloves
it's possible I mightn't have thought about her hands,
about what they've done. Ah, at last a little . . . just a little
anger,' he said to himself, listening to his heartbeats. 'I've
taken enough time about it.'

'Well,' said Camille sadly, 'well, what are you going to
do? Perhaps you haven't decided yet.'

'Oh yes. I've decided,' said Alain.

'Ah!'

'Yes. I can't come back.'

'I quite understand that there's no question of your
coming back today.'

'I don't want to come back.'

'Not at all? Ever?'

He shrugged his shoulders:

'What does that mean, ever? I don't want to come back.
Not now. I don't want to.'

She watched him closely, trying to distinguish the false
from the true, the deliberate irritation from the authentic
shudder. He returned her suspicion for suspicion. 'She's
small, this morning. She looks rather like a pretty shop-
girl. She's lost in all this green. We've already exchanged
a fair number of useless remarks.'

In the distance, through one of the arched arcades, Camille caught sight of traces of the 'alterations' on one side
of the face of the house; a new window, some freshly-
painted shutters. Bravely she threw herself into the path of

danger: 'Suppose I'd said nothing yesterday?' she suggested abruptly. 'Suppose you'd known nothing?'

'What a superb woman's idea,' he sneered. 'It does you honour.'

'Oh,' said Camille, shaking her head. 'Honour, honour. It wouldn't be the first time that the happiness of two married people depended on something that couldn't be owned up to ... or wasn't owned up to. But I've got the idea that by *not* telling you, I'd only have made things worse than ever for myself. I didn't feel you were ... I don't know how to put it.'

Hunting for the word, she mimed it by clenching her hands together. 'She's wrong to draw attention to her hands,' thought Alain vindictively. 'Those hands that have sent someone to their death.'

'After all, you're so awfully little on my side,' said Camille. 'That's true, isn't it?'

That struck him. He had to admit, mentally, that she was right. He said nothing and Camille insisted plaintively in a voice he knew all too well.

'Isn't it true, you hateful man?'

'But, good God!' he burst out. 'That's not the question. The only thing that can possibly interest me – interest me in *you* – is to know whether you regret what you've done, whether you can't stop thinking about it, whether it makes you sick to think of it. Remorse, good heavens, remorse! There does exist such a thing as remorse!'

Carried away he got up and strode round the circular lawn, wiping his brow on his sleeve.

'Ah!' said Camille with a contrite, affected expression. 'Naturally, of course. I'd a million times rather *not* have done it. I must have lost my head.'

'You're lying,' he cried, trying not to shout. 'All you regret is that you didn't bring it off! One's only got to listen to you, to look at you with you little hat on one side and your gloves and your new suit – everything you've so carefully arranged to charm me. If you really had any regret, I'd see it in your face. I'd feel it!'

He was shouting now, in a low grating voice, and was no longer quite master of the rage he had fostered. The worn stuff of his pyjamas burst at the elbow and he tore off nearly the whole of his sleeve and flung it on a bush.

At first Camille had eyes only for the gesticulating arm, extraordinarily white against the dark block of the yew hedge.

He put his hands over his eyes and forced himself to speak lower.

'A little blameless creature, blue as the loveliest dreams. A little soul. Faithful, capable of quietly, delicately dying if what she has chosen fails her. You held *that* in your hands, over empty space . . . and you opened your hands. You're a monster. I don't wish to live with a monster.'

He uncovered his damp face and came nearer to Camille, trying to find words which would overwhelm her. Her breath came short and her eyes went from the white naked arm to the bloodless face which was no less white.

'An animal!' she cried indignantly. 'You're sacrificing me to an animal. I'm your wife, all the same! You're leaving me for an animal!'

'An animal? Yes, an animal.'

Apparently calm now, he hid behind a mysteriously informed smile. 'I'm perfectly willing to admit that Saha's an animal. If she's really one, what is there higher than this animal and how can I make Camille understand that? She makes me laugh, this barefaced little criminal, all virtue and indignation, who pretends to know what an animal is.' He was prevented from going further by the sound of Camille's voice.

'*You're* the monster!'

'Pardon?'

'Yes, you. Unfortunately I can't exactly explain why. But I assure you I'm right. *I* wanted to get rid of Saha. That wasn't at all admirable. But to kill something that gets in her way, that makes her suffer – it's the first idea that comes into a woman's head, especially a jealous woman's. It's perfectly normal. What's abnormal, what's monstrous, is you. It's . . .'

She was struggling to make herself understood and, at the same time, pointing to certain accidental things about Alain which did indeed suggest a kind of delirium: the torn-off sleeve; the trembling, insulting mouth; the cheek from which all the blood had retreated; the wild crest of dishevelled fair hair. He made no protest and did not deign to defend himself. He seemed lost in some exploration from which there was no return.

'If I'd killed . . . or wanted to kill . . . a woman out of jealousy, you'd probably forgive me. But since I raised my hand against the cat, you're through with me. And yet you don't want me to treat you as a monster.'

'Have I said I didn't want you to?' he broke in haughtily.

She looked at him with terrified eyes and made a gesture of impotence. Sombre and detached, he watched the young, execrable gloved hand every time it moved.

'Now for the future, what are we going to do? What's going to happen to us, Alain?'

He was so brimming over with intolerance that he nearly groaned. He wanted to cry out: 'We separate, we keep silent, we sleep, we breathe without the other always there! I'll withdraw far, far away – under this cherry-tree for example, under the wing of that magpie. Or into the peacock's tail of the hose-jet. Or into my cold room under the protection of a little golden dollar, a handful of relics, and a Russian Blue cat.'

He mastered himself and deliberately lied:

'But nothing, at the moment. It's too soon to make a . . . a decision. Later on, we'll see.'

This final effort to be reasonable and sociable exhausted him. He tottered as soon as he took the first steps when he got up to accompany Camille. She accepted this vague conciliation with hungry hope.

'Yes, of course. It's much too soon. A little later on. Stay where you are, don't bother to come with me to the gate. With your sleeve, people will think we've been fighting. Listen, perhaps I'll go and get a little swimming at Ploumanach with Patrick's brother and sister-in-law. Because the mere idea of living with my family at this moment . . .'

'Yes, do that. Take the roadster,' proposed Alain.

She flushed and thanked him too effusively.

'I'll give it you back, you know, the minute I get back to Paris. You may need it. Don't hesitate to ask me for it back. Anyway, I'll let you know when I'm going and when I get back.'

'Already she's organizing it all. Already she's throwing out the strands of her web, throwing out bridges. Already she's picking up the fabric, darning it, weaving the threads together again. It's horrifying. Is that what my mother admires in her? Perhaps, after all, it's very fine. I don't feel any more capable of understanding her than of making things up with her. How completely at ease she is in everything I find insupportable. If she'd only go now, if she'd only go away!'

She was going away, carefully avoiding holding out her hand to him. But, under the arcade of clipped trees, she dared vainly to brush against him with her ripening breasts. Left alone, he collapsed into a chair and near him, on the wicker table, suddenly, like a miracle, appeared the cat.

A bend in the path and a gap in the leaves allowed Camille to see Alain and the cat once more from the distance. She stopped short and made a movement as if to retrace her steps. But she swayed only for an instant and then walked away faster than ever. For a while Saha, on guard, was following Camille's departure as intently as a human being. Alain was half-lying on his side, ignoring it. With one hand hollowed into a paw, he was playing deftly with the first green, prickly August chestnuts.

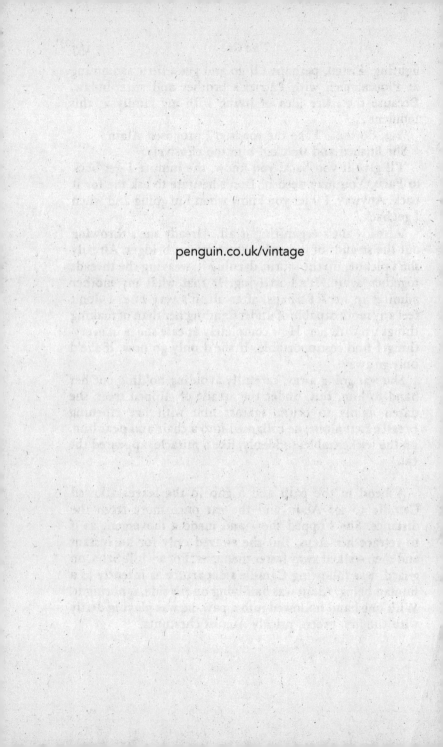